Mississippi Folk and the Tales They Tell

· Myths, Legends and Bald-Faced Lies ·

DIANE WILLIAMS | *Photography by Susan Allen Liles*

The History PRESS

Published by The History Press
Charleston, SC 29403
www.historypress.net

Color cover images: Photographs by Susan Allen Liles.
All other cover images from Marion Post Wolcott, Library of Congress, Prints & Photographs Division, FSA/OWI Collection.

First published 2014

Manufactured in the United States

ISBN 978.1.60949.932.7

Library of Congress CIP data applied for.

To those who have stood by me, encouraged me, uplifted me and loved me unconditionally, you will always have a special place in my qalb. *Thanks to my sister Alice Brown for all the funny jokes; Jerry L. Jenkins for being such an incredible artistic soul-friend and brother; Linda Johnson and Oni Lasana for being my encouragement; Willa Brigham for the gift of massage during the stressful times; Fellowship Bible Church for unconditional love; Susan Marquez and Benjamin Morris for being the first readers; and Nellie "Mack" McInnis—you are my music and melody.*

Contents

Contents

Introduction

I'm a "road hog," and I've been traveling Mississippi listening and talking with people from all corners of the state for over twenty-five years. I started out as a transplant from New Jersey, by way of Texas, where I met my husband. When we first came home (Madison, Mississippi, his home of birth), I was very apprehensive. Of course, I had heard all the stories about my new home, especially the ones about the racial tensions and prejudices. I soon learned that I would be welcomed from the very moment I boarded the plane with a baby in my arms. The people on the plane from Houston, Texas, to Jackson, Mississippi, were very helpful in making sure that I was able to properly breastfeed my child without exposing the activity. But it could have been that they were in no mood to hear a baby cry for any length of time. Either way, I relaxed, and I'm still enjoying the ride today. I feel right at home here, and even my accent can attest to that. One moment, I'm talking southern, and the next minute I'm being teased about my accent and everyone guesses that I must originally be from the New York area, which is true. I grew up in Newark, New Jersey, fifteen minutes outside of Manhattan, New York. I wear it as a badge of honor that says to anyone listening, "Don't mess with me. I don't take no stuff. I'm a mover and shaker, a workaholic," and I'm still known as a "city-slicker."

Because I was not familiar with the state and its culture when I first arrived, I decided to get out on the road and explore—just me and my small child. We got involved in volunteer activities and soon became acclimated. I learned that no matter what my station in life, I would always be identified not as Diane Williams but as Ray's wife. I was referenced by a term of endearment—"a stay-at-home wife"—and the community would only respond to my identification as Ray's wife. I found this to be perplexing. It seemed that I did not have an identity of my own. Ironically, I am no longer married, but I have come into my own as a professional storyteller, author and mixed media fiber artist. People now find me multifaceted, and some may go so far as to say that I am a jack-of-all-trades, to which I jokingly respond, "No, it's all about storytelling in a variety of formats. I am a narratologist!"

I have told stories in every corner of the state and in almost every type of venue imaginable—so much so that people now refer to me by saying, "Oh, you're the storyteller." As I gained more experience over the years, I expanded my interests and started working with communities to help them collect their stories and value what they have to celebrate with one another. Sometimes those story gatherings have been healing balm to communities with racial tensions and identification issues. But more often than not, the stories that I've helped communities collect have been the vehicle for helping them remember a time gone by. One of my favorite sayings is this: "I help communities to uncover invisible artifacts."

I learned to collect oral histories from the University of Southern Mississippi and the Mississippi Humanities Council (MHC). I worked out in the field along with folklorists and other oral history collectors in rural communities such as New Hebron, Columbus and Prentiss, Mississippi. Those field trips helped to leave an indelible mark on communities by way of the local performances we created in celebration of the stories that were collected, the university archival storage, the creation of booklets and—my favorite—the landmark that is now positioned in concrete in front of the Okolona Carnegie Library. If you visit the site, I promise you'll either ask, "What is that thing on the ground? Do they worship the devil here?" or you'll ask someone, "What's the story behind that thing?" Well, along with professional storyteller Rebecca Jernigan, the Okolona Chamber of Commerce and the architecture department at Mississippi State University, I wanted to create a labyrinth on the grounds of the public library but soon learned that there wasn't enough space around the library for this project. So that's why there is a "thing" on the ground. It is a metal plate embedded into the concrete. Children worked with Mississippi State University's architecture department to re-create the stories that were gathered and sculpt and cast the images into metal. The flat, circular metal plate depicted childlike images of home, cemeteries, people, animals, landmarks and a time gone by. Images relating to the stories that were told of the old movie theater, the swimming hole and the underground well are all finely crafted by children to the best of their abilities and ages.

It is the hope of this writer that since the storytellers came to town, there is a deeper appreciation for the invisible artifacts. People have learned from one another. They've heard one another's stories, folklore and even some bald-faced lies—and they've learned to respect one another because of their stories. At first, they were afraid to share. They had kept the stories hidden in their hearts or whispered, sputtered and "juked" on front porches. The stories would come out, whispered around kitchen tables while women stirred pots and men slugged beer. The stories flowed and were whispered in church fellowship halls and at garden clubs, but never—never—would the stories be told in gatherings where the entire community could learn about their history, fortitude and perseverance.

That's the way it is in Mississippi, and that's the way it has always been. That is what has made the folktales and folklore of this state so elusive. Mississippi is surrounded with folklore, those stories that identify us by place and tradition, but trying to uncover the folktales of Mississippi has been something I've wanted to do for many years.

Folktale and folklore evoke strong images, but understanding the differences and similarities depends on who is explaining. It's important to explain to the reader that this book is about both folktales and folklore. What is this thing we call "folktale"? I found a definition that I like a lot. It states that a folktale is "a tale circulated by word of mouth among the common folk." By God, that's exactly what this book is about! It can also be described as being "a tale or legend originating and traditional among people or folk, especially one forming part of the oral tradition of the common people." The dictionary defines it as "a characteristically anonymous, timeless tale circulated orally among the people." It is very much a part of the oral tradition, and that is why I had to get in my car and become a "road hog" again, getting out in the field to talk with the people. I wanted to capture those stories that have been so well documented in the minds, in the hearts, in the ears and on the lips of Mississippians.

I've spent a year traveling and talking with rural and city residents about their stories. There is an incredible common thread even though one cannot identify Mississippians as one particular culture. The way they do things, the way they refer to how it was done in other places. They actually name the place as if history marking was important. They say things like, "In Natchez, they do it this way or they say it that way, but up here (and they say that with an element of mustered pride with syrup dripping off of it)…This is the way we did it!" Even though the title of this book is *Mississippi Folk and the Tales They Tell*, naming individuals is not as important as the stories because the stories have traveled with their suitcases from one place to another. The intimate details are what give communities ownership of their story, no matter where you go and who you talk to in the state.

Folklore consists of legends, music, oral history, proverbs, jokes, popular beliefs, fairytales, stories, tall tales and customs that are the tradition of a culture, subculture or group. It is also the set of practices through which those expressive genres are shared. It can be discussed in relation to four areas of reference: artifacts, oral tradition, culture and behavior (ritual).

The goal of this book is to evoke more stories. I envision you reading a story, laying the book down and gathering with a group of folks to talk about the ways in which you or your community might have intersected with the subject matter. At least, that's what happened when I went out into the community. As one person would tell me a story, it would dovetail into another story on that same subject, told slightly differently, adding elements that continued to build enthusiasm and interest while rising to a crescendo of laughter and joy that could be referenced and retold so many different ways by different people. So the challenge for me was to take all those accounts and blend them so that they resonated as if echoing off a mountain down into a valley and back up on the hills again.

Earlier, I stated that Mississippians could not be identified as one particular culture. The state is composed of regions. There are the Coastal Meadows, Pine Hills, Jackson Prairie, Loess Hills (Bluff Hills), North Central Hills, Delta (Yazoo Basin), Flatwoods, Pontotoc Ridge, Black Prairie and the Tombigbee Hills, and there are different things happening in each of those areas that make them unique. Their uniqueness can be experienced through the foods residents eat and the music they listen to, the community activities that take place and the people of renown who come from those communities.

I used to travel in my car with an arboretum book on trees because the foliage and trees are so different in each part of the state. In North Mississippi, you might find ginkgo, and in South Mississippi, you will find the longleaf pine. This may not seem so important at first glance, but once you start listening to the stories, you'll learn that it is integral to the lives of those living in any of those areas. This is more important than politics. As a matter of fact, if you want to see a fight break out, just talk about redistricting the political landscape.

It is the hope of this writer that people will find some of the stories interesting in a way that only the oral tradition could evoke. I'd like to be one of the first people to tell you to put the book down at that point and share your own version of the story motifs. Share your culture, traditions, habits and lifestyle. Then pick the book up again and have yourself a good laugh at some of the idiosyncrasies that you will find within these pages.

Ivory-Billed Woodpeckers in Madison County

I encountered one of the first stories when I started writing this book while talking with a craftsman who worked with metals. I watched as Lyle Wynn hammered hot iron into tools or decorative shapes that looked a lot like birds and other animals. He told me about growing up in Mississippi and wanting to go hunting. The opportunity came when he got his first car. In a state whose very nature is rural, this was an opportunity for him to explore the great outdoors and observe nature. There was one hunting adventure that was very special to him, one that he never forgot. He was around fifteen or sixteen years old and was sitting in a tree stand with a muzzleloader in anticipation of hunting deer. Two birds flew by him and soared up into a pine tree, where they started pecking. He watched as these two giant woodpeckers did their work. The wings of each bird had white patches and spanned over thirty inches. Their bodies were black with a red-and-black crest on their heads. They also had white patches along their backs and necks.

This young man was well versed in nature and the wildlife that frequented the woodland communities. He understood that the ivory-billed woodpecker (*Campephilus principalis*) was becoming extinct and that the population had started shrinking considerably since the late 1800s. Twentieth-century sightings by bird-watchers were only noted to have taken place in a few locations in the entire United States.

This youthful hunter knew that he had witnessed two of the most incredible forest birds of the wild. Although the pileated woodpecker is a similar specimen whose vocal abilities are represented by a clear, high pitch series of piping calls that lasts several seconds, the ivory-billed woodpecker has a more nasal tooting "*kent*" or "*hant*" sound that resonates much like a toy trumpet and is often repeated in series. When the bird is disturbed, the pitch of the "*kent*" note rises. The pileated woodpecker's sound is a shorter call that sounds like "*wuk, wuk*" or "*cuk, cuk*" and with which the bird marks its territory or boundary.

The young man immediately told the game warden who worked in that area that he had seen ivory-billed woodpeckers. He went on with excitement, "There were two of them! Those things were huge! They were incredible!"

The warden responded in a nonchalant slow drawl, "Oh, those are just those pileated woodpeckers."

Certainly, that game warden didn't realize that Lyle had made an incredible discovery.

Twenty years later, there was an article in the statewide newspaper, the *Clarion-Ledger*, with a picture of those ivory-billed woodpeckers. It was said that $1 million was given to a man to determine whether the birds were really extinct. This species of bird faced extinction due to a loss of habitat. Woodpeckers serve the woodland community by making rectangular holes in tree wood. Those holes have served as shelters for owls, bats, pine martens, ducks and swifts.

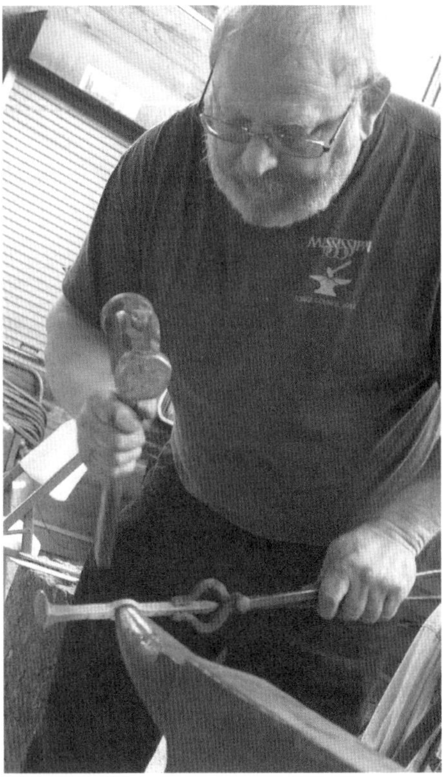

Lyle Wynn grew up and witnessed another sighting of ivory-billed woodpeckers at the Ross Barnett Reservoir up around Highway 43 in Madison County. Other sightings have been recorded in Arkansas and Louisiana.

Those interested in documenting the presence or possible extinction of these birds needed someone with credentials to verify whether there were any ivory-billed woodpeckers still around, but they strictly ignored Lyle. I wonder why.

For Whom the Bell Tolls in Rural Madison County

In the days before radio, bells rang throughout communities to make announcements, herald the arrival of prominent visitors or celebrate events such as weddings, births or deaths. Many Mississippi communities have stories to tell about those "for whom the bell tolled." The church bells pealed announcements, happenings and convenings to all the people who lived within earshot.

There was a time when itinerant preachers passed through an area wanting to share their message for a small agreed-upon compensation. The local church layperson would ring the bell, and religious community members who might possibly be interested would send children over to the church to get more information. These traveling preachers, evangelizing throughout the region and looking for a friendly place to settle, would make sure that they were the talk of the town by way of the bells affirming their arrival. A small group would assemble in a tent revival setting to receive the message. If the preacher entertained and engaged, he would be welcomed back. If not, someone might be standing at the tent entrance to usher him out of town.

Circuit riders had been around since the frontier days of the United States, and the riders' purposefulness ended just prior to the Civil War. They were always welcome, and word would spread from city to city by word of mouth and through the ringing of the bells.

When there was a death in the area, the bell would toll. Tolling was done by pulling on a rope and holding it so that the rhythm could be controlled.

Some bells had a special device that held them in place while someone struck them with a toller. The length of time the bell would toll depended on the age of the deceased. Church bells can be pealed, chimed, dinged or tolled, but tolling is done by making a slow, thoughtful ringing of the bell.

In country schools, a four-inch hand-held bell would ring to begin the day and to announce the time for recess.

The designs of these bells were selected to serve specific purposes. This was back in the day prior to bells activated by electricity. You can still find some country churches that ring handheld bells to announce the transition between Sunday school class and church service or to mark time on the hour. Today, one very well may find a bell on a hotel clerk's desk. If the clerk is absent from the front desk, all one would have to do is ring the desk bell, and that would alert the clerk to stop whatever he or she is doing and come to assist.

During the days of the flourishing southern plantations, large bells would sound to announce times for specific activities for slaves, sharecroppers or tenants (depending on the era). Farmers listened and obeyed the rooster, but large farms and plantations depended on the bells to announce the time to awaken and get the work day started, take a break, get back to work and quit at the end of the day. Family farms often had a bell sitting on the front porch, and the women of the house would ring the bell to announce dinner to the family and farm workers out in the field.

Bells also announced emergencies, such as a neighborhood fire. Each community had its own language and vocabulary when it came to the purpose for ringing bells. The old steam-engine trains even rang bells when they slowed down and rolled into town.

The ringing or tolling of bells could also cause an upheaval of gossip, if misunderstood. One case in point occurred in a small town when the local tombstone craftsman made a headstone for Ms. Abigail. During her lifetime, she was notorious for lying about her age. She dyed her hair, wore clothing that was more suited to a woman half her age and practiced good health and nutrition in an effort to keep her figure. Ms. Abigail always had a glow about her. Admired by all, she became the talk of the town when she died. No known cause of death was listed on her death certificate. Everyone was talking! But ironically, they were not talking about her surprised demise. They were buzzing all around town about how old she was.

Mr. Rogers, the tombstone maker, listed Abigail's date of birth as 1908, and her death was listed as 1971. But Rogers was seventy-five, and he remembered going to school with Ms. Abigail. He knew his place, and he knew his job. His job wasn't to prove her life span. His job was to do exactly as requested by the family or else he wouldn't be paid. He was a bit concerned, though, because he had to edit the dates on more than one headstone because of the community gossip. It was this undercurrent of unconstrained conversation that made people question whether the deceased had been around longer than suspected.

Well, the real trouble started when the hearse rolled up to the Baptist church. When the bell let out its first hallowed chime, the community started counting—one, two, three…sixty-two, sixty-three—everyone held their breath, but the bell pealing ceased, the ringer retired and the funeral service began. There was a buzz in the congregation as the parishioners read the obituary. Everyone was comparing notes. Five people had been asked to speak on Ms. Abigail's behalf. Three of them were God-fearing citizens of the community, while the other two were old and had lived their lives gossiping like hoot owls in the night by phone, by candle light and by any means necessary. The first three people to speak on behalf of Ms. Abigail did so without incident. The fourth orator, John Johnson, stood before the crowd and took his time looking around and calculating how people would respond to what he had to say. John was a man whose character was expressed in his everyday lifestyle. He raised pigs. So when he finally spoke, he said, "Wooo wee!" It was a sound similar to the "sooey" or "soo wee" sound he made when calling his pigs. "It's time somebody set the record straight. Ms. Abigail never married, but she was loved by all. She has brothers and sisters, but there is no way that she, being the eldest of her siblings, could be younger than the ones sitting here in this sanctuary today. No one wants to admit it, but Mr. Rogers, the tombstone maker, has a job to do. He has already made Ms. Abigail's headstone, but let's be fair to him and let him know that he might as well change the date on the headstone right now!"

Mr. Johnson, in the middle of the funeral service, declared, "I'm calling this meeting to order. Who in this room has the earliest remembrance of Ms. Abigail?"

Before he could say another word, folks started raising their hands to speak. The preacher and deacons were afraid things would get out of order and didn't know what to do. A few minutes later, it was determined that Ms. Abigail was at least ten years older than the sixty-three years listed on the obituary. People started sharing pencils up and down the aisles crossing out the birth year on their copy of the obituary. Everyone wanted to get and keep the record straight. Very few people discard obituaries. They keep them for the sake of archival memory, and no one wanted an inaccurate account. It was a cardinal rule of gossip to make every effort to accurately keep dates in order.

Finally, Mr. Rogers spoke up. There were gasps all around the room from the prudish ladies of the church because, although he was paid to do a job, he could attest to the fact that Ms. Abigail wasn't the only one who had lied about her age.

"We are about to lose sight of reality, and I'm standing here today, in front of Abigail's casket, thinking out loud. I cannot tell a lie. I am seventy-five years young. Abigail and I were classmates back when we were children. She loved life and enjoyed it as much as one can. But we ought not to allow her to go to her grave with this lie."

At that moment, family members stood and shouted, one after the other. "Wait a minute! Wait a minute! Abigail can do whatever she wants to do!"

Mr. Rogers retorted, "Abigail is dead!"

The pastor looked at the deacons, and they all looked at the bell toller. Something had to be done before a fight broke out. The bell toller ran up to the tower and started pulling the rope as hard and as fast as he could, making the bell ring furiously. The pastor stood up and said, "Enough of this, congregation! Enough! Our dear Abigail is gone, and we should be ashamed

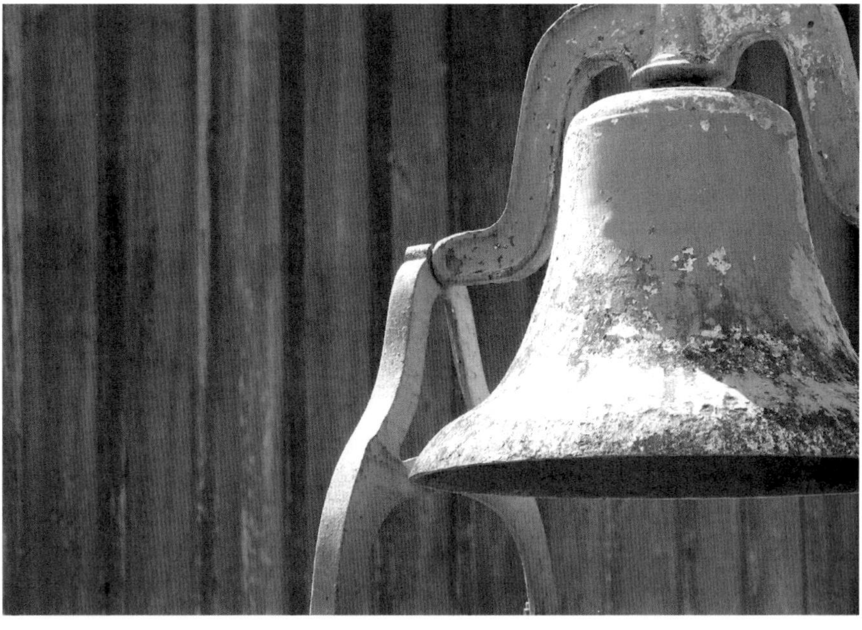

of ourselves. What she did was wrong, and it has caused this community to perpetuate a lie. I'm closing out this service by asking you all to repent and ask the Lord to forgive you."

For those individuals who did not attend the funeral service that day, they stood in their doorways befuddled and scratching their heads. The talk in the town after that was not about Abigail. No, that situation had been resolved. The talk was about the bells. After the funeral, the bell toller had rung the bell so feverishly to set the record straight that it confused the townspeople and word spread far and wide, with folks asking one another, "For whom does the bell toll?"

Frog Gigging in Rolling Fork

Tommy Shropshire grew up in the Mississippi Delta, and with a lathering of pride, he enjoys sharing stories of frog gigging around Rolling Fork. Rolling Fork is a small town not far from the Mississippi, South Arkansas and North Louisiana borders. Rolling Fork boasts of having around 2,500 people living on less than 1.5 miles in Sharkey County.

Along with other boys in the community, Tommy recounted with a tinge of youthfulness rising from underneath his baseball cap as he touched the brim, he captured frogs everywhere you could imagine in and around Rolling Fork.

"Lord, we started out as kids and soon became authorities on how to catch them and where to find them," he said, and he dutifully noted the best ways to eat them.

Frog gigging involves taking a long pole-like object with forked prongs on the end of it and actually stabbing it into the frogs. It was not the most humane way of capturing frogs.

"I rank frogs as the number-one food there is. People say it tastes like chicken, but it is *not* just like chicken—it is more like a cross between chicken and fish. It's fine eating, especially when you get a bullfrog about two feet long. When you stretch 'em out from the head to its feet, it is as big around as your fist," Tommy said with a wink of his left eye.

Tommy and his gang would gig frogs from a small boat along the little creeks and streams around town. The frog gigs looked like broom handles with three prongs on one end. The soft mud made gigging the frogs a slippery task, and once you got the gig into one, it was a little messy pulling it off.

The boys' methodology evolved from gigging the frogs to using a little clamp-like contraption, sort of like a mousetrap. They would spread it apart and put it upside the frog and then clamp down on the critters, but the contraptions didn't work as well as the gigs did. However, they did allow the frogs a few more minutes of merciful prayer time.

As Shropshire and his boys grew a bit older, their methods for catching frogs changed from rendering the tender mercies of the mousetrap devices to shooting .22 rifles at the critters.

"We'd put on blue jeans and tennis shoes and go out into the swamp. I had a little battery-operated light on my baseball cap, and we'd walk around out in the swamps where the snakes were wading. We didn't have no waders or boots back in those days. We didn't have to worry about creatures such as alligators. There weren't any alligators back then in and around Rolling Fork. The alligators were basically gone at that time, but since then they've come back. We'd wade around in the swamps all night long, shooting snakes and frogs and then going back to fetch the frogs and put them on a fish turner, tie it to our belts and pull it along."

Shropshire had a classmate whose dad was the superintendent of the school district. After a night of catching frogs, they would go to his house around one or two in the morning and wake his dad up. In a sleepy drawl, Shropshire's buddy's dad would say, "You didn't shoot anything bigger than a frog tonight, did ya? Now you boys go get cleaned up and get you some sleep."

The boys would get up bright and early that next morning and take the frogs through a ritual of cleaning them and frying them up in a pan. The ritual ceremony would end with the chomping down on fried frog legs, with toast and jelly. It was a tradition of every good ol' boy in Mississippi to eat them that way.

"It don't get no better than that! That's good stuff!" Tommy told me.

As the boys matured, their techniques for frog gigging got better and better, and their boats got bigger and bigger. They ventured out to the river streams, like the Sunflower River, Little Sunflower and Yazoo, and they would grab the frogs with their bare hands. Someone would be stationed in the front of the boat, someone would drive the boat and someone else would hold up a big spotlight. They would ease slowly up to the bank near the frogs, and the person in the front of the boat would actually grab the frog, hold him tight and then turn around and put him in a sack or ice chest—anything that would hold the frogs. That became the best way to get frogs.

Sometimes they would get pretty close to catching a snake. There would be a snake snuggled unseen right next to a frog, or they would get up to the bushes and there'd be snakes that would crawl up into the boat. Those were times of mayhem as the guys jumped out of the boat seeking safety. Tommy testified that this sort of adventure didn't happen very often.

Back in those days, there were just water snakes. They would leave you alone if you didn't bother them. The only poisonous snakes one would encounter out there in the Delta swamps of Sharkey County would be the cottonmouths. If one of those snakes took a bite out of you, it would leave you some very nasty venom to deal with. But the Shropshire gang don't have stories of ever getting bitten. With no accidents, they all survived and lived to tell about it.

It seems that the methods for frog gigging or grabbing progressed in every community as young boys learned to figure out what worked best. It became a favorite pastime.

"We didn't know what drugs were…television wasn't that big a thing…we didn't have any electronics. It was the baby boom era, so we kids just went around doing things together," said Tommy.

Tommy Shropshire was sixty-five when he told this story. He started frog gigging around the age of twelve or thirteen and gigged on through college. When asked if girls ever frog gigged, his response was, "Not intentionally!"

Tommy dated a girl from Terry, Mississippi, and when he'd go pick her up, her brother would say, "This is a good evening as any to go frog gigging, don't you think so? Let's go."

So Tommy ended up going frog gigging with the girl's brother instead of on a date with the girl. As a result, he said, "The girl and I didn't last long because frog gigging was a better deal. The boys and I had a blast! It kept us out of trouble, and we got good food to boot!"

As with all stories, one thing leads to another. Tommy had other hunting adventures that took place after he got his driver's license; back in those days, you could shoot rabbits at night, but that has since been outlawed. The boys would ride around at night in pickup trucks with spotlights and shoot the rabbits. Squirrel hunting was also a big deal to young men growing up in the 1950s. Squirrel hunting in Mississippi and even nationally is not what it used to be. There are plenty of squirrels, but the children are not as interested today. Young people find other sports and activities to get involved with now.

Squirrel connoisseurs will tell you that the squirrel is mostly dark meat, and if cooked just right—moist and tender—its texture is something like that of chicken, but it also has a wild game flavor. You can fry it, and some

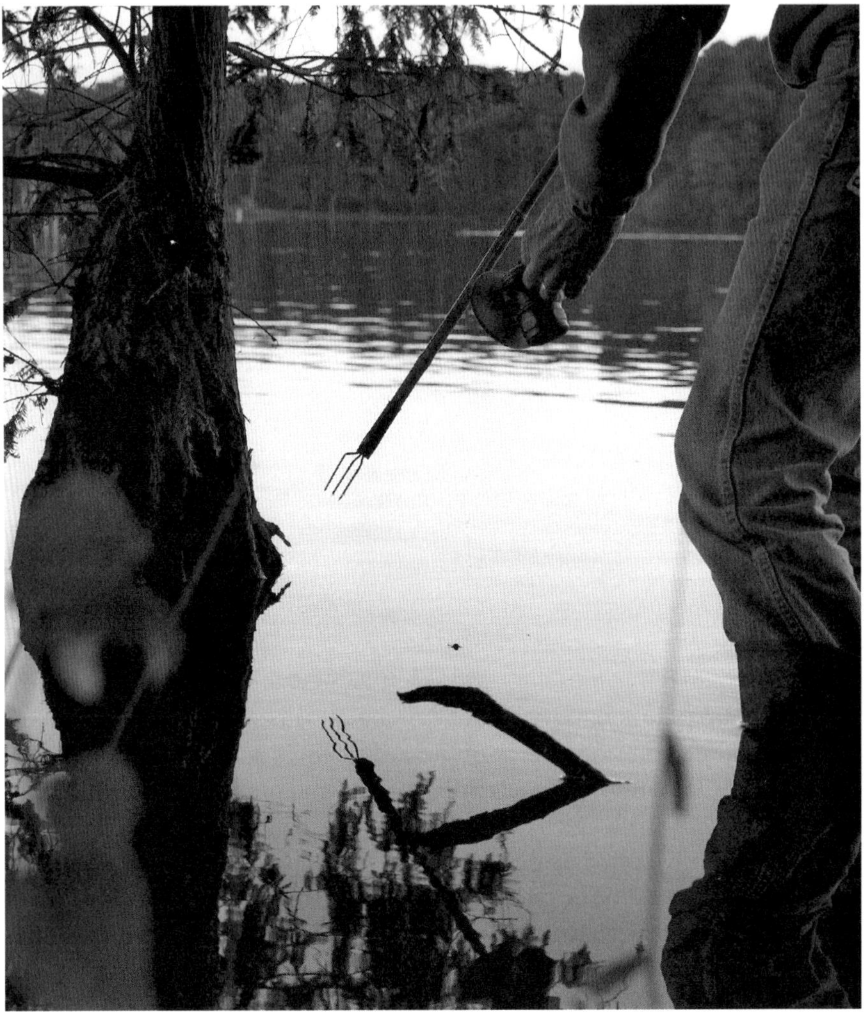

people make jerky out of it, but the most popular way to cook it is to make squirrel stew. Some people have even confessed to cracking the skull and eating squirrel brains. Tommy said that he has done some things in his life but he could never do anything like that. It just never appealed to him.

"We'd go to camp, and there would be a big old pot of stew with squirrel heads floating around in it. That just doesn't sound appealing anymore."

Squirrel brains are probably extremely high in cholesterol. It is bad for you, but it evidently tastes good if people are eating it.

There is still plenty of deer hunting going on. Deer hunting in Mississippi is and has always been the biggest sport for young hunters.

Old Jim Gordon's Gold in Willoughby

By Ralph E. Gordon

Back before the Civil War when Dixie was a nation,
There lived a man on the red-clay land who owned a great plantation.
Old Jim Gordon was his name,
A stash of gold was his claim to fame.
And when the Civil War was fought,
Jim took his gold to the banker's vault.
But the banker's vault he did not trust,
Cause Old Jim knew of the Yankees' lust.
He returned there to his farm,
And hid his gold from Sherman's arms.
Sherman took the best and burned the rest, then went to rob Old Jim.
A sly old cuss, he never made a fuss; He just outsmarted him.
"I have no stash, just take my cash, then go and leave me be."
Old Sherman took one look at Jim and marched on to the sea.
Until this day, old timers say, the gold will always be,
Beneath the ground near the old ghost town known as Willoughby.
So bring your shovels and bring your spades,
And dig the ground where the gold was laid.
Before you dig, please let me warn,
Some say this legend's just a yarn.
Crops were lost at an awful cost
From men digging little holes,
But not a single dime did they ever find of Old Jim Gordon's Gold.

Govan Gordon moved from Alabama to Newton County, Mississippi, in 1832 with his sons, Jim and Eli. He acquired 2,300 acres of land where he farmed and raised horses. The older son, Jim, developed a passion for fast horses and began breeding some of the finest in the area. Jim's horses gained a reputation throughout Mississippi and surrounding states for their speed and agility. When the Civil War broke out, Jim struck a deal with the Confederate government to supply horses to the army. Gold was the only money Jim Gordon would accept as payment for his horses. He did not trust the Confederate dollar and trusted the Yankee dollar even less.

In the spring of 1863, Colonel Benjamin Henry Grierson of the Illinois Cavalry conducted a raid straight through to the heart of Mississippi. By the time the colonel and his party arrived in Newton County, he was in desperate need of fresh horses. Jim Gordon's reputation proved to be his worst enemy. Grierson, having knowledge of Jim Gordon and his horses, raided the Gordon farm and took them all. Unlike Sherman, Grierson was a compassionate man who saw no need to destroy private property or take private property without compensating the owner. Grierson left his horses with Jim as payment for the ones he took. A year later, Sherman confiscated those same horses. But horses were not all Sherman was looking for from Jim Gordon.

Old Jim, as he was sometime called, knew that Grierson would not be the last Yankee to raid Mississippi. After Grierson's raid, Jim hitched his wagon and mules and carried his gold to a bank in Meridian, Mississippi, for safekeeping. The banker eagerly gave Jim a tour of the bank and the safe, assuring him that his gold would be in good hands. But when he offered Jim Confederate money in exchange for the precious metal, Jim refused to make a deal with the banker. He returned to his farm with his gold and buried it, never to reveal the location—not even to family members.

In the spring of 1864, Union general Sherman of the United States Army conducted what is known as Sherman's Meridian Campaign. The general and some twenty-five thousand troops entered Newton County near Conehatta in the southwest part of the county. From there, he drove on to Meridian and then turned and circled back and entered Newton County near Union, which borders Neshoba County to the north.

Sherman visited Jim Gordon, where he reclaimed the horses that Grierson left with him. The general further demanded that Jim turn over his gold. When Old Jim denied having any gold, Sherman burned his house and all his farm buildings.

Sherman left Jim's place and rode five miles to Boler's Inn in Union, where he spent the night. The next morning, he ordered his men to spare the

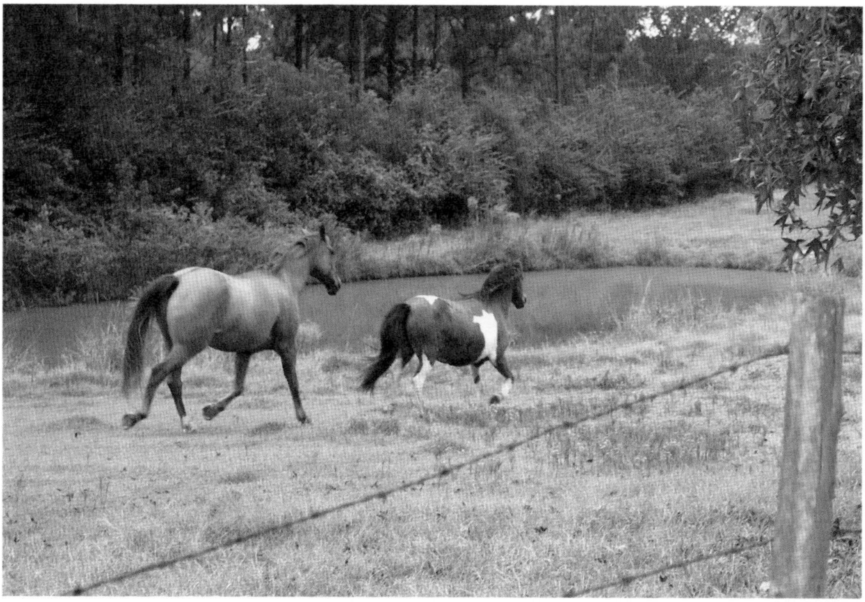

town of Union because of its name. Boler's Inn still stands in Union today. The old stagecoach stop was restored and converted into a museum by the Foundation for the Restoration of Bolers' Inn, a nonprofit organization. And Jim Gordon's gold remains buried somewhere in the red clay not far from where Sherman slept on the night of February 24, 1864.

After the war, Colonel Benjamin Grierson organized and led the Buffalo Soldiers of the Tenth Cavalry Regiment from 1866 to 1888.

What happened to Jim Gordon's gold?

Does anyone ever go there to search for the gold?

What happened to the site itself?

The Gunfight at Willoughby Crossing

By Ralph E. Gordon

Down by the railroad station lived a man called Big Lonzo.
He and Uncle Gene were feuding and one of them had to go.
Both were quite bullheaded. The feud was all about land.
They met at Willoughby Crossing with their shotguns in their hands.
The women folks were praying that the Lord would make it right.
And that he would see fit to intervene and stop this deadly fight.
Make no mistake about it, Uncle Gene he was the best,
With his knife or with his shotgun or with his deadly fist.
His brother Oscar told him, "Now listen to me, Gene.
The law will surely come for you. You've got to keep it clean."
Give the man a fighting chance before he has to die,
And when the sheriff comes for you, you'll have no cause to lie.
The day was cold and windy and death was about the air,
Then Gene Gordon closed one eye, just to make the gunfight fair.
The women's prayers were answered as buckshot went astray,
Neither man could kill, you see, for a foot poor pinch of clay.

In 1912, farmer Gene Gordon and his neighbor, farmer and store owner Big Lonzo Harrison, became involved in a landline dispute. Some say the feud began when the train ran over and killed one of Gordon's cows. Gordon's cow broke through Harrison's fence and eventually wandered out onto the railroad tracks, where it was killed by an oncoming train.

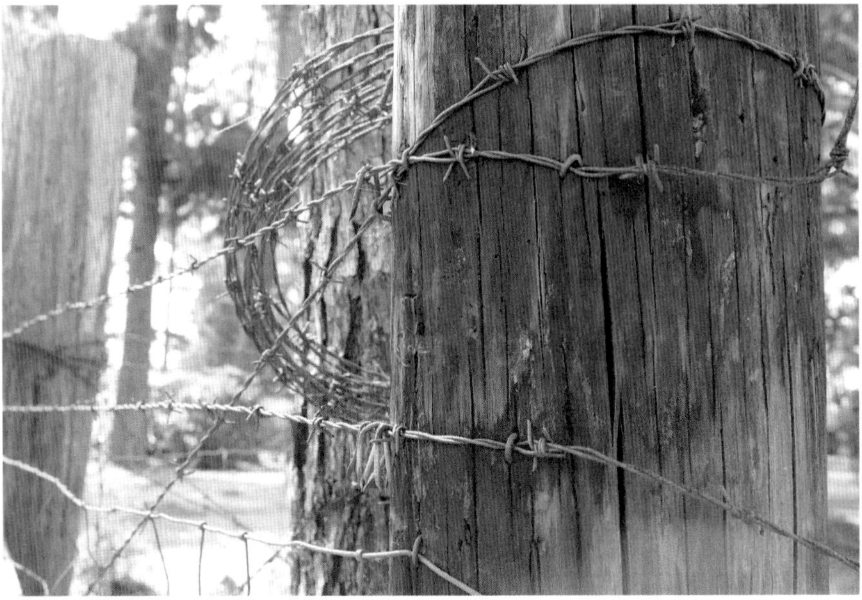

When Gordon found his milk cow dead beside the tracks, he discovered that the fence had been moved. Gordon claimed Harrison had moved the fence (without his knowledge) over onto his property, giving his own farm slightly more acreage.

Gordon confronted Harrison, who denied moving the fence. When the two men could not come to terms in a peaceful manner, they agreed to fight a duel to resolve the feud once and for all.

According to witnesses of the duel, Harrison's bullet missed its intended target but hit Gordon's gun barrel. Harrison was also lucky. Gordon missed too but shot Harrison's hat off his head.

After protests from their womenfolk, the two men came to their senses and settled the feud in court.

THE GHOST TRAIN OF LITTLE ROCK

By Ralph E. Gordon

In eighteen hundred and forty nine,
Tracks were laid for the M&M Line.
Mud and Misery—she was called back then;
Built by the sweat and the blood of good men.

For more'n a century trains hauled riders and freight.
Not a single time was the trains ever late.
They hauled brothers and cannons for the Blue and the Gray,
And saw many young men meet their judgment day.

The trains carried sailors and soldiers to two world wars,
America's bravest rode in cattle cars.
Women folk would wait by the tracks,
Praying she would bring all the young men back.

A ghost steam engine still runs the line,
You can hear her whistle blow around suppertime.
But the fact is that men came and took up her rails years ago.
But the M&M whistle still wails and blows.

A man named Kirby is her engineer,
She squeaks and she rattles as she's drawing near.
She's hauling cotton, cattle, coal and grain,
You can even hear her brakeman yodel and sing.

Some are skeptics and don't believe,
But I've heard her whistle on a summer's eve.
If you have faith, you can set your clock,
By that Old Ghost Train to Little Rock.

The poem "The Ghost Train" is a composite story. It could be about any one of so many abandoned rail lines across America, but because so many people claimed to have heard the Little Rock train's whistle blow years after the line was closed, the ghost train to Little Rock is the poem's main focus.

Older people in the communities along the old line claim they have heard a steam whistle blowing late in the afternoon. The younger generation professed to have heard an air horn that sounded like one of the newer diesel locomotives. Whether it was a steam whistle or air horn, the legend of the ghost train to Little Rock was born.

The poem is fictional. However, the trains were running across the nation during the early part of the twentieth century. The term "doodlebug" was given to the first successful motorcar: the Union Pacific #1 McKeen motorcar built in late 1904–05. The poem "The Ghost Train" is symbolic of any train that served the community and has now been discontinued. Little Rock, Mississippi, existed in 1849, but there was no railroad service there until the early 1900s, when the M&M line came through.

The thirty-mile Meridian and Memphis (M&M) Railroad line, which connected Meridian and Union, Mississippi, had many stops along the way during the early years of operation. But because of the large number of passengers who boarded in a town called Little Rock, Mississippi, a tiny hamlet about nine miles out of Union, the train's nickname became the "Little Rock Doodlebug." It started out as a trolley-like commuter car. You could stand on the track and flag the train down. The first trains pulled only one passenger car. Passengers loved riding in the Little Rock Doodlebug, while doodlebugs around the country filled a practical need in communities at the turn of the twentieth century.

On March 15, 1913, the first commercial freight moved along the tracks in the Little Rock Doodlebug. It was a boxcar that carried groceries for a general store, and it traveled only about four miles. By April, a steady flow of lumber loads was arriving from a sawmill fourteen miles away, near the midpoint of the line at Suqualena. The first passenger train to come on the scene had three to four passenger cars and carried five hundred people from Union to Little Rock along with a number of freight cars that traveled approximately six miles total over the course of a day. Across the nation, stories are told of incidents on the passenger/freight trains known as doodlebugs.

The line between Union and Meridian was abandoned, and the rails were taken up in the late 1970s, leaving a long and lonely strip of land to return to nature. This was a far cry from the fanfare and celebration accompanying the first doodlebug to run through Mississippi. It has been said that twentieth- and twenty-first-century bike riders assert that their bikes still rattled for a ten-mile stretch along a strip of road where the train once screeched and hooted.

Prior to the 1900s, folks in the northern part of Newton County traveled by horse and buggy or mule and wagon, or sometimes they used the oldest form of transportation known to man—they walked. When they traveled, it was probably out of necessity. In 1905, things began to change. Progress was on the way.

The Mobile and Ohio Railroad (M&O) laid tracks running north and south through the heart of the county, connecting Union and Decatur, Newton to the south and Philadelphia to the north. Eventually, connections were developed on into Memphis, St. Louis and Chicago. During that same year, the Meridian and Memphis Railroad laid tracks connecting Union and Meridian. These ribbons of steel changed not only the way folks traveled, but they also changed their way of life forever.

Some thirty miles of tracks were laid between Union and Meridian, using mostly manual labor to handle the heavy crossties and rails. Men swung nine-pound hammers in the heat of summer and in the cold of winter, driving spikes into treated oak crossties. For the most part, mule-drawn dirt slips were used to build the roadbed. What few steam-powered machines they used in building the line were confined to the newly built tracks, unlike the bulldozers and rubber-tired earth movers of today.

Eventually, a larger steam engine replaced the doodlebug. It pulled one passenger car and as many freight cars as needed. In the early years, a train was made up of two or three freight cars, along with a caboose. Diesel-electric locomotives replaced the steam engines on the line in 1946. The more powerful diesels pulled as many as seventy cars. They hauled everything from canned beans to chemicals and cotton bales. Perhaps the most exceptional piece of cargo shipped into Union by rail was a prefabricated house kit from Sears and Roebuck, delivered to a Mr. Nutt around 1915.

It cost twenty-five cents to ride the train from Union to Meridian. The doodlebug's first stop on the route from Union to Meridian was in Willoughby, about three miles out. There was a cotton gin there, one of

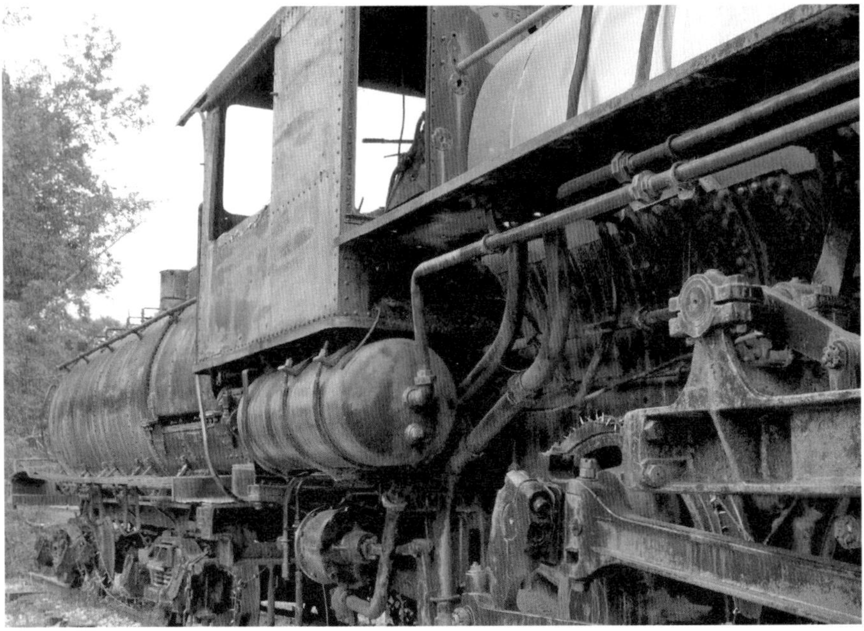

the largest in Newton County. The next stop was Perdu and Duffee in Newton County. The train also stopped at Shambersville and Suqualena in Lauderdale County before reaching its final destination in Meridian. The trip took about three hours. The last passenger train departed the Union depot in 1951.

The whistle of the Little Rock Doodlebug is but a distant memory to the people of Willoughby and Little Rock—or is it? Some folks claim they can still hear its lonely whine echoing across the red clay hills and marshy hollows, late in the afternoon, about the time the train would be making its return trip to Meridian.

How Poplarville Got Its Name

There used to be a joke that traveled the Poplarville grapevine. It has been said there were more Smiths than there were pine trees in Pearl River County—and there were a lot of pine trees. The person who shared this joke, Bill Restor, says that his mama was a Smith, so he was a bona fide representative who could testify firsthand that there were a bunch of Smiths along a 3.9-mile stretch of land on the outskirts of Poplarville.

In small rural communities in Mississippi, there are untold stories left on the grapevine that would explain how there could be a large brood of family members with the same name in such small communities. No doubt there are schoolhouses where children sit side by side and inevitably learn that they are related to one another. Today, many of the rural churches maintain a tradition of two to three family groups that serve on every committee; brothers and cousins are on the deacon board, and the mothers of the church are all sisters, cousins, aunties and nieces. Details that would clarify the intricacies of the family tree are never shared. Simply stated, on any given day, you might hear someone say, "Chile, I don't know how Jim is your cousin, but he is!"

Old Man Smith had a pile of kids, and for some reason, they were all named Jim. There was Black Jim and Red Jim. There was Poplar Jim, Goat Jim Smith and others. He did have one son that he called Red John. Now, Poplar Jim was not named because he was so popular. He was named that because there were poplar trees growing in his yard. Each Jim had a different identifying term connected with his name, but they were all named Jim, nonetheless.

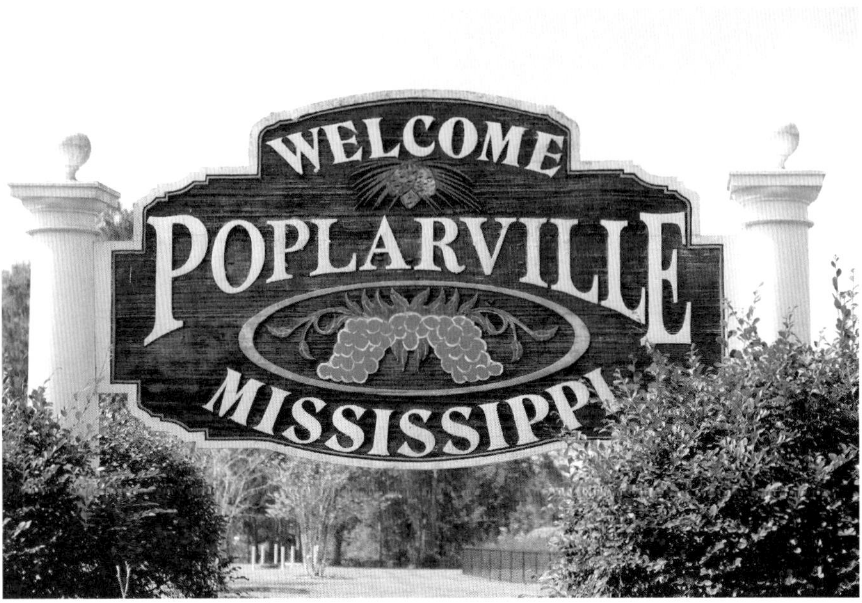

In and around Poplarville, folks just seemed to lack originality when it came to naming. There were a bunch of Stewarts around those parts as well, and some of the sons had names like Goat and Rat.

Poplarville was named after Poplar Jim Smith, who gave the town the land that the courthouse sits on (that little bitty dab of a plot of land), and he also gave the town the land where the Baptist church sits. There were other plots of land that can be attributed to Poplar Jim Smith's generosity, as well, and so the town was named Poplarville, after him.

The town was settled approximately 150 years ago. Folks don't seem to be sure of the exact date. They mark the town's birth date by landmarks such as the United Methodist Church, which was started in 1879. Poplar Jim also gave the city the land that the United Methodist Church sits on. Some would say that butter wouldn't melt in his mouth, but he was very generous beyond a doubt.

Some of the nicest people you'll ever meet live in Poplarville today. It is one of those towns where everyone knows everyone else's story.

Poplarville Has a Haunted House

Many people talk about haunted houses, and if you've heard one bump in the night, you've heard one too many. In Poplarville, there is a haunted house. All the children in town know about it, and all the adults whisper about it, but nobody will come right out and admit it.

It wasn't built one hundred, fifty or even forty years ago. It was built when things changed in Poplarville, when the roads became different, and the couple who built the home had it constructed pretty close to where an old situation was that one cannot really say a lot about. The fact is that someone had been murdered there.

The house was lovely, with beautiful new furniture. The lady of the house belonged to all the clubs in town, and all the club members were offered an opportunity to come and see the beautiful house.

Mary Etta Moody was one of the club ladies who saw the interior of the house. As beautiful as it was, she shivered whenever she talked about it. When you entered through the front door, the first thing you would notice was that the house was cold. It was cold all the time, even in the summer.

The couple didn't live there long. There was something about that house that seemed to have shattered their marriage, and so they moved out and went their separate ways.

It wasn't long before another couple moved in. They stayed there a good six months and then moved out. They moved because they kept hearing strange sounds. The neighbors heard it, too, but they didn't say anything because they wanted somebody else to buy the house. They felt that if they said anything, the house wouldn't sell.

Then another couple moved in. They stayed the longest—a full three years. They thought they heard people walking around in the house, along with screams and yelling. They heard something that sounded like people dragging things around. It must have been unnerving because eventually, they, too, moved out.

The next couple to move into the house attempted to remodel it. The neighbors were hopeful. But the couple lasted only six weeks before they departed in fear. After that, the house remained empty, and it never sold again.

Someone reported that the sounds that came from the house may have been one of the El Chupacabra, the ghost-like hairless zombie dog that had been spotted around Pearl River County. Although no one in Poplarville has seen the creature (with the exception of a few individuals with wild imaginations), the sounds that reportedly emanated from the El Chupacabra were unmistakable. It certainly provides a logical explanation for the ghost sounds and bumping around that the residents and neighbors heard coming from the house, but it was pure speculation.

The legend of the El Chupacabra dates back to the 1970s. The name El Chupacabra means goat-sucker because the creature has been purported to attack livestock and suck the blood of goats. The creature could have been a coyote or a wild dog with mange. As long as there were residents in the house, the creature hid in the wooded area behind the house and bumped around foraging for food in the trashcans at night. The creature

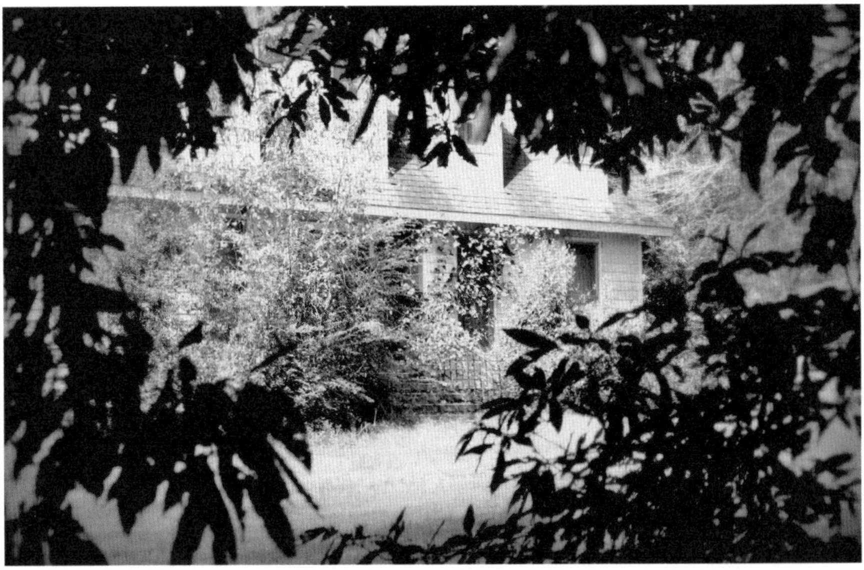

may have hid underneath the house when it was unoccupied. There were farms in the area, and the animal may have managed to stay alive by killing farm animals.

If folks had talked about it aloud rather than whispered and gossiped, someone with a rational mind could have called the animal control officers and put a stop to the ghost house mystery.

The local women still whisper today, "Don't you dare go and tell anybody that I said this now, but that place is haunted. That's the loudest screaming and raising sand going on over there that you'd ever heard in your life…"

Marijuana and Moonshine in Poplarville

Mr. Douglas H. Strahan tells of a time that, unbeknownst to him, he was growing marijuana. He always wanted to be a farmer, so when he was able, he bought himself a twenty-one-horsepower Kubota tractor and started an okra patch.

Okra is the state flower of Louisiana. If you lived in Louisiana, your refrigerator would be stuffed with okra. Although Mr. Doug lived in Mississippi, the green prickly vegetable made an impression on him, so he planted twenty rows of okra, and the plants grew to be about twelve inches. His field was looking good, and like any good farmer, he came to know and appreciate every stalk. Then he noticed that the stalks alternated from green to dark green. The odd-colored stalks just stood out, and it couldn't be denied that there was something different about this okra patch.

Mr. Doug was familiar with the appearance of marijuana because he had been a customs agent. Marijuana plants and okra plants look a lot alike. To his shock and surprise, he began to realize that every other stalk was a marijuana plant, and he wondered what sort of Brer' Rabbit had gotten into his garden patch.

Now, there were some mischievous boys who lived across the fence, and he became suspicious. He pulled up all of the okra and marijuana and put it in a pile and burned it, and that was the end of his okra farm. There was just one problem: because of the nature of the burning plants, anyone within a certain radius could not only smell the aromatherapy, but they would reap the benefits as well.

Mississippi State University (MSU) has a federal marijuana farm that is legendary in Mississippi and has been growing "pot" legally for years. MSU has an ongoing medical marijuana program that would make hardcore drug dealers jealous.

Mary Etta Moody of Poplarville tells the story of an elderly neighbor, Miss Jane, who nurtured beautiful plants from seeds that someone had sent to her. She fertilized them, and they grew to become pretty and mature.

One day, a man representing the authorities came to her house and said, "Miss Jane, we will have to take all of your plants."

She said, "Please don't! They are going to bloom pretty soon. I want to get the flowers and seeds from them so that I can replant."

He said, "You can't have them, ma'am. I'm going to have to take them because those are marijuana plants."

Miss Jane was a religious woman, and it almost killed her to find out that she was harvesting drugs. She just about died when the man told her that what she was doing was illegal. She had an acre of marijuana growing, and she didn't even know what it was. She thought the marijuana looked like hibiscus. Mary Etta concluded her story by saying, "We are really very law-abiding citizens here in Poplarville."

Mary Etta Moody knows a lot of the stories from the Poplarville community. She remembers a time when Pearl River County had plenty of moonshiners, some of whom were really famous for their distillery skills.

One time, there was a fellow living in Carnes who had some really fine moonshine. He delivered his brew in tanker trucks. It was probably some of the best whiskey around. It was like Doctor Tichner's on speed! It was very hot and could knock your teeth down your throat. Once the word got out that he was concocting something that powerful, his production increased and so did his deliveries. Unfortunately for him, the federal boys had pegged him to "go down." Somebody alerted him to the fact that the authorities were onto him and would be coming soon. The moonshiner cleared out, leaving the moonshine and the still.

Have you ever wondered where the name "moonshine" comes from? It may have had something to do with what men did by the light of the full moon out in the woods at night. Moonshine ingredients include water, flaked maize, crushed malted barley and sugar. The remaining recipe ingredients are usually a family secret, as is the methodology of the distilling processes. If the moonshiner wanted to ferment it quickly, he would throw in a dead varmint like a possum or rat. Most legitimate distillers steered away from that sort of thing. But suffice it to say that making moonshine is a dangerous enterprise.

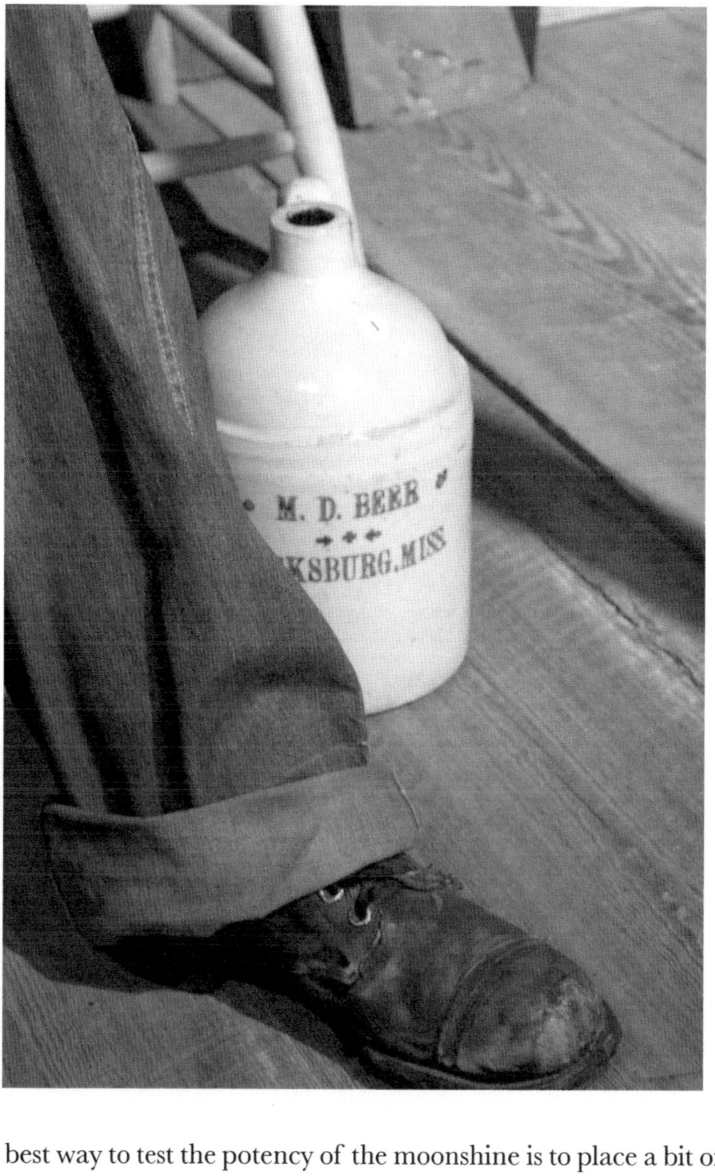

The best way to test the potency of the moonshine is to place a bit of it on a spoon and light it with a match. Poof! Good moonshine burns with a blue flame, and tainted moonshine burns with a yellow flame. Don't ask how one would know whether that is true. Just take the good folks' in the community's word for it.

The Big Chicken Fight in Wiggins

Bill Rester grew okra down in the Wiggins community. One day, he and his sons were harvesting their crop. It got hot outside, and the boys got their tempers in a pretty bad skunk. By the time they made it back to the house, the eldest one knocked the youngest one down. Bam! He hit the ground. Bill saw the whole thing, and he didn't like it one bit.

He took his knife and cut one of the vines off the okra and stripped it down, telling his sons, "We gonna bring this thing to a head, boys. I have had enough of y'all getting into it all the time."

He told the eldest boy, "You always beating up on your younger brother. We're gonna change that up a little bit. You're gonna fight. You're gonna go four or five rounds, depending on what y'all can stand, and Hyram, you can guard yourself, but you better not swing a lick. If you do, I'm gonna wear you out and we're gonna start over."

Those boys had been worn out before with one of those old-fashioned wear-outs from the okra vine. Hyram didn't want any more of that.

Bill said, "Let's get after it."

The youngest boy, Drew, had a strong left punch. He loved the idea of taking the lead in a fight with his brother.

Bill said, "Hook up."

They went after it. Bap, bap, bap. Hyram was doing a good job of guarding himself. Drew went to beating on Hyram, whose face turned red and his ears got puffy.

Hyram begged, "Turn me loose on him, Daddy! Turn me loose on him!"

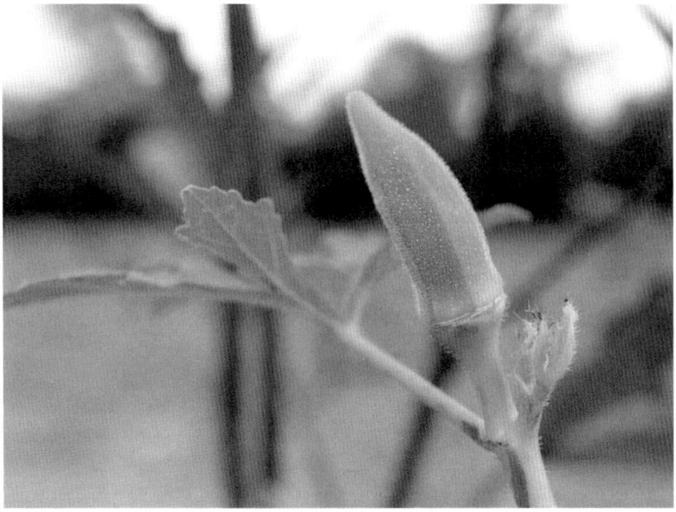

Bill shouted, "Break! Now, back up! Drew, you want some more?"

"Yes, sir, Daddy."

"Let's go another round."

They went back to fist fighting again.

Hyram said, "Turn me loose on him, Daddy! Turn me loose!"

Bill broke them up again and then let them go another round. They were both getting dinged and were in pretty bad shape. Drew was getting pretty winded from doing all the punching.

Bill said, "Drew, are you ready for me to turn Hyram loose?

"I don't give a flip what you do!"

He was fired up. He was whooping his big brother.

Bill surprised everyone when he said, "Okay, Hyram, you're turned loose. Start your round."

Flip! Hyram knocked Drew down, and in a flash, it was all over with. The moral of the story is that Drew got knocked down in a fight. But he got to whip Hyram in three rounds. Hyram couldn't hit him back because Bill wouldn't let him, and that incident changed Drew forever. It stopped the confusion in the house.

After that, if Bill came in and the boys were "yang-yanging," he'd say, "Y'all want to go outside and let Daddy watch?"

Nope! Neither one of them wanted to fight. They'd both got whipped in that situation. They still "yang-yanged" a little bit, but they never fought again. So okra is good for something other than eating, especially when you can make a point with the vines.

Bill Restor's Childhood Possum in Wiggins

No one can tell this story like Bill.

I was number five, raised in a big family. I had three older brothers and one sister. I got roughed up pretty bad as a kid, but I loved having folks around me. Our family lived out in the country just outside of Poplarville. All the kids in the neighborhood went to school. My brothers and sister went to school. I was at home with my mother, and I just about drove her crazy. I wanted somebody to play with—a little brother is what I was asking for.

I went to my mother, and I asked, "How do you get a little brother?" and she just looked at me.

I said to my dad, "Where do little brothers come from?"

My dad said, "You get them from little tree stump holes. If you want a little brother, you go out by the tree stump and look in the stump hole and you'll find a little brother. Just look in the hole every day."

I did exactly what my daddy said. I had a little stick horse named Dixie, and I got on that stick horse and rode it down past the pasture. When I arrived at the stump hole, I turned Dixie into a stick—just for a minute. I'd turn her upside down and stick that stick into the hole and rake the leaves back and forth. I did that for I don't know how many months. I'd ride that little horse down there, and I'd hunt in those leaves. I really wanted me a little brother, somebody to love, somebody for company.

One day I was raking those leaves back and forth, and something wiggled. I got down on my knees, and I'd raked those leaves back and I uncovered a half-grown possum about a foot long. If you'd seen the teeth on that thing—it looked like a monster. I was thinking, boy, I have found me a little brother, and I said to myself, "Boy, that thing is ugly. He's ugly as my oldest brother, but boy, he's my little brother."

I reached down in that stump hole, and I grabbed him. I forgot about my little stick horse Dixie. I left it lying in the leaves. I grabbed that little possum up, and all I had on was a pair of hand-me-down overalls: no drawers, nothing but those overalls and I remember one strap was unbuckled. I clasped my little brother up to my chest, and he grabbed on to my ninny with his teeth. I was nothing but skin and bones back then. He clamped down on me and wouldn't turn loose for nothing.

I walked back to the house holding him and clasping that little old sweet thing. When I got home, I used my foot to open the screen door. My mama looked, and I was a sight. I had tears running down through the dirt on my face. There ain't nothing dirtier than a little white country boy that's been playing out in nature. I had little streaks coming down my face, and I was holding that little brother tight.

Mama said, "Son, what's the matter?"

I said, "Mama, I found me a little brother, Mama. He's ugly as my brother Larry, but he's my brother and I love him."

She asked, "What's he doing?"

I said, "Right now, Mama, he's getting ninny. But if he ever gets through, he's going to be a weaned little son of a gun, I can tell you that!"

Murder Creek, the County Crossroad

Stone, Forest and Pearl River Counties

Murder Creek is not just a memory. It is a bona fide place of criminal activity. Down around Poplarville, off Highway 26 and the surrounding areas, where the red wolf would roam along the rivers with the foxes, coyotes, deer, turkeys, rabbits and birds, you would think it would be a peaceful place. But folks got restless around this area. The Wolf River is named after the red wolf that journeys from the Piney Woods to the Gulf of Mexico. Along the river, you can find tall cypress and gum trees and tidal marsh. At one time, the Choctaw and Creek Indians graced the landscape with their native lifestyles of gleaning from nature and the earth. The river provided plenty of fish, and the area grew as people settled in. This area is known for its longleaf pine and hardwood trees, which served as a resource for ship builders and farmers.

The Wolf River is a source of beauty along the Mississippi landscape, but it also has its darker side. The understanding of what went on around the Wolf River has a lot to do with the enterprise of trees, lumber, shipping and farming. There were things that went on in those woodlands from which families today try to separate themselves. There is a reason for that. Names can be recalled, but specific landmarks designate the spot where colorful outlaws and gangs committed crimes. So much of that happened "back in the day" off Highway 26 that the area was named "Murder Creek," and it is still called that today. It is said that actions of the rival gang members of the Wage and McGrath families are one of the reasons the creek was given its name. But there were other families who ravaged and caused trouble for the Murder Creek community as well.

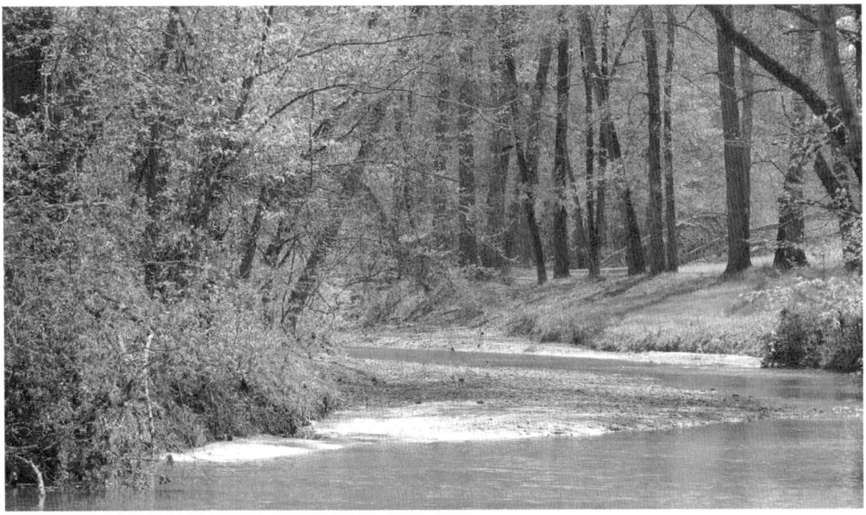

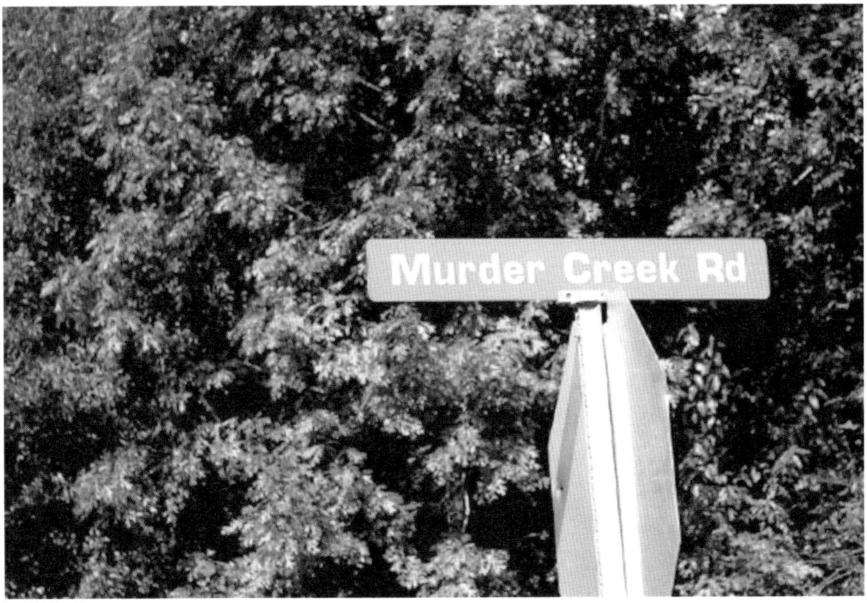

It is said that the Colemans were murderers and liars—pure evil. There is an area where Stone, Forest and Pearl River Counties come together, and there are four corners where the Colemans used to fight chickens and dogs. The sheriff would come, but he couldn't come across the county lines. Chicken and dogfights also took place down in Necaise, too. Hancock County is another place where chicken fights used to take place.

Bill Restor and his daddy were out plowing the field one day. Bill wanted to go fishing, and he told his daddy so.

His daddy said, "Yahoo! That's the best idea you've had all day, boy!"

His daddy told him that on Friday, everyone shut down from plowing at noon, and they would start oiling their guns and sharpening their knives for Saturday. They were getting ready for those chicken fights, and they would gravitate from chicken fighting to knife fighting. If Tommy and his daddy were going to go fishing, they needed to do it before the weekend brawls started.

Word has it that the evil Colemans had an ongoing feud with some people outside of Poplarville. They went to a church on what is now known as Murder Creek Road, and they lined up all the parishioners and shot them, one by one. Folks learned the hard way that you didn't want to get into a disagreement with this group of rabblerousers.

The Colemans still live around Poplarville. However, the Colemans of today are pretty nice people, and they don't claim to be kin to the murderous folks by the same name. There are some nice Colemans living in Carnes as well. Pistol Ridge was home to those reprobate Colemans.

The Turpentine Shack in Pearl River County

Bill Restor's great-granddaddy Frederick and his brother-in-law, Jackson, packed their rifles and took them wherever they went. They lived out beyond the stockyard of Poplarville. The brothers-in-law became fast friends and spent a lot of time turkey hunting together well into their old age.

There weren't a lot of deer in the woods in that area back in those days, but there used to be turpentiners in the deep part of the woods, and they used to carve hash marks and put spigots in the trees from which resin would be extracted. It would drip into buckets that were hitched to the trees. There would be nearby shacks scattered throughout the woods, and generally the turpentiners would hire African Americans to live in the turpentine shacks around Poplarville. They'd monitor the flow of the dripping resin and keep the trees freshly slashed. They'd put the resin in containers and store it in the shacks until it could be distilled into turpentine at the factory.

When Frederick and his brother-in-law would ride through the woods, they would often stop to get a drink of water. There was a spring by one particular turpentine shack where they'd stop. One day, they saw buzzards sitting on the roof of the turpentine shack house, and as they'd rode up to get a closer look, two little black boys came darting up and ran into the house. When Frederick and Jackson peeked inside the shack, they were surprised to find the mother in bed. She had clearly been dead for weeks, and her face was unrecognizable. The little boys had been out in the woods living in that shack alone. The father couldn't be found.

Frederick and Jackson reported it to the turpentine company immediately. The little boys were very young and had been there without anybody to

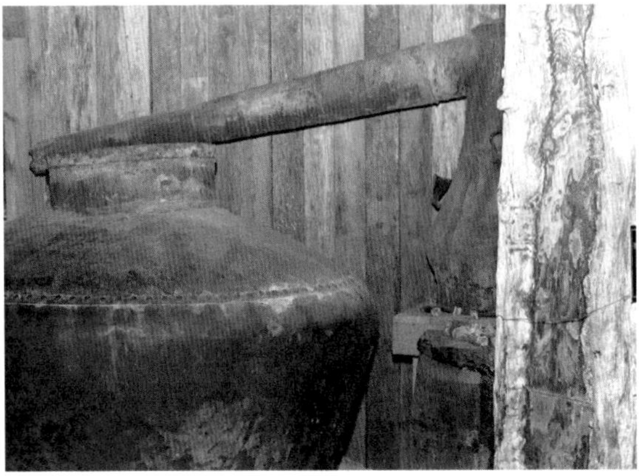

care for them. Frederick and Jackson picked up the two boys and put them on their horses and rode them home to live with them.

Granny Sue (Bill's grandmother) was part Native American. She was an herb doctor. Granny Sue doctored on the one little boy, and he lived, but the other little boy died because he hadn't eaten in a very long time. The one who lived was raised up in the house with Bill Restor's daddy. His daddy and the boy actually played together as children, and he attended the Crosby School with Bill Restor's daddy. The Restors raised this little black kid and took care of him as if he were their very own. Bill recalls his father telling him about the times when Granny Sue would make that black boy hug a tree, and she would take a whip to him.

Bill said, "That's terrible, Daddy!" But his daddy said that Granny Sue did the same to all the children.

As a child, the little black boy from the turpentine shack ended up going to school along with the white children. As Bill tells it, there was integration in a few small communities in Mississippi way before you'd hear people talking about trying to institute it.

The boy from the turpentine shack grew up and was sent off to college, and Bill met him one time. He came to visit the family in a big Cadillac when Bill was a small boy. He told them that he had become a minister and lived in the Chicago area. Bill doesn't remember the preacher's name, but he's determined to find out more about that story. He has a picture of the minister as a little guy in his teenage years.

Bill has a picture of the two brothers-in-law standing with their rifles in their hands. He doesn't know when the picture was taken, but he imagines that it was taken some time after the Civil War. The gun in the picture is an LC Smith. Bill's eldest son has that pistol now. His brother was shot in the stomach with it. The Gibson family lives in the Poplarville area, and they tell that same story and have a copy of that same picture. The Restors and Gibsons are working together to uncover the rest of the story.

Milking Cows in Carnes

When Ernestine Thompson was a young girl, her responsibility was to milk the cows. There was a lot of milking to do, and there were a lot of children in the family who could pitch in and do it. Usually there were at least three cows being milked at any one time. Ernestine's favorite cow to milk was named Butterbean, so named because it was caramel-brown and white in color and looked like a speckled butterbean. One morning, Ernestine was milking that cow when suddenly she heard something making a noisome buzzing over the sound of the squirting milk. She looked around and noticed that it was a big bug, the kind that tumbled in the poop and rolled it up in a ball and buried it.

It was Ernestine's recollection that these were real pretty bugs, fluorescent blue, green and red, and there is an account in a book somewhere that says that there was a time when the Egyptians thought the bugs were so beautiful that they made jewelry in the image of those bugs. Ernestine thought the bugs were pretty fascinating, too, but it bothered her to think the Egyptians thought they had something that was special to them because she thought the bugs were special too. In her opinion, they were exclusive to south Mississippi.

Well, she was sitting there milking when the bug landed on the cow's head. She kept milking because she was almost finished and wanted to get through before the bug upset the cow. That bug just kept crawling around and around until it got up close to that cow's ear, and lo and behold, that bug went right into that ear and Ernestine had to jump up and get out of the way

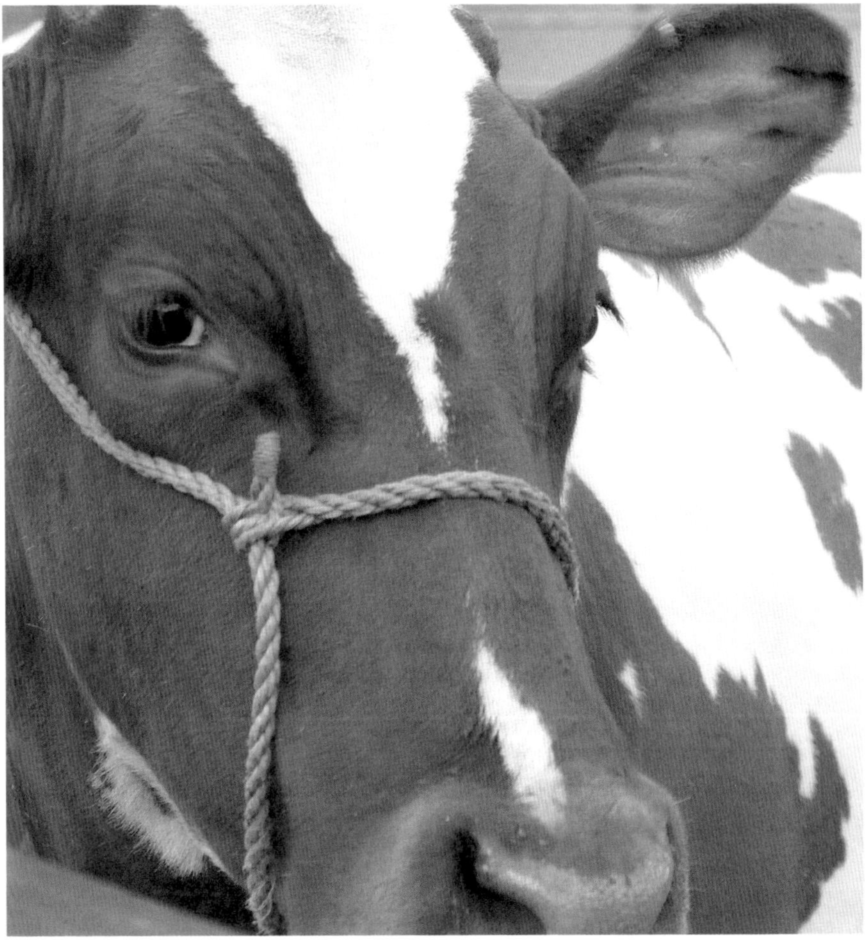

before the cow had a fit. About that time, the bug plopped right down in the middle of the milk bucket. He evidently went right into one of the cow's ears and came out the udder!

The Wiggins Pickle Factory

The story of Lorraine Craig and her cucumber farm bears a resemblance to the story of many rural residents whose lives intersected with the Brown and Miller Pickle Factory in Wiggins. The pickle factory was the regional hub of activity in south Mississippi for folks living thirty to fifty miles or so from the Gulf Coast.

The Brown and Miller Pickle Factory provided Lorraine with a job she could do while staying at home with her children while her husband was away working. The year was 1975. She was excited. She had planted two cucumber gardens. She was going to grow and pick cucumbers to sell to the pickle factory in Wiggins. It was a major industry in that neck of the woods. She watched with eager anticipation as the fine little seeds grew and flourished. Finally, the day came when they blossomed and turned into little cucumbers. "It was harvest time! How wonderful! How good could it be!" she thought.

On any given day, before the sun came up, she had all six children fed and dressed. Her kids were twelve, eight and four, along with two three-year-olds and the baby, who had just turned two. Once dressed, they then headed out to the garden with a blanket, water and snacks. Lorraine carried the two-year-old and one of the three-year-olds. The older boy helped to carry the second three-year-old. The youngest boys were not at all happy and howled all the way to the garden.

It was a quarter-mile walk to the cucumber patch. The grass was pretty tall in the pasture, but the family wasn't concerned at all about snakes.

Lorraine grew up as a "country girl" and figured that if the snakes had any sense at all, they'd be running for safety away from her and the six children. The dew was still heavy on the vines, and the family was dressed in long pants and long shirtsleeves to prevent the "pricklies" from getting to them. Working out in the hot sun caused their clothes to become crusty with sweat, but nothing slowed their progress. At high noon, they were ready for a break and walked the quarter mile back to the house for lunch before returning to the garden.

After a few days, the family members adjusted to being bent over for hours at a time. Without counting the time that it took to eat lunch, they averaged seven to eight hours of picking the large garden of cucumbers and three to five hours of picking in the smaller one. Lorraine alternated picking in each garden every day because if they didn't pick all the cucumbers, they would eventually be too large to sell.

The saying in that region was that the cucumbers would literally grow overnight. You had to run out there and keep picking them off early, but as soon as you left the field, it was as if you could hear them growing behind you. The cucumbers on the vine were very prickly, and the sap that grows on them was almost like tar. It was *very* sticky.

Spiders grew among the rows of cucumbers, and they were worse than snakes. The spiders would get on the vines overnight. They would curl up in web wads, and when you'd go to pick the cucumbers, the spiders would come out of the wads. The vines grew to be twelve inches, up to your knees. You had to reach down in there, and your arms would be covered with dew and vines and the "pricklies" from the sticky leaves.

On the short days when there wasn't as much picking to do, Lorraine washed clothes and cooked in preparation for the times when they would be in the garden all day. The two older boys were a big help, and Lorraine gave the babies an *A* for effort. Even the two-year-old toted ice cream buckets filled with tiny cucumbers to the end of the road and helped to pour them into the big bags. At the end of the day, her husband would come home from his job, they'd load the bags of cucumbers into their truck and off they'd go to Wiggins the next day to sell them.

By the time Lorraine and the rest of the Craig family made their way to the pickle factory in Wiggins, there would be a line five miles long. The heat boiled at around ninety-five degrees on any given day, and they were a sight to be seen, coated with the sticky, prickly mess and caked mud from the cucumber garden. They always went straight to the pickle factory after picking because of the long lines.

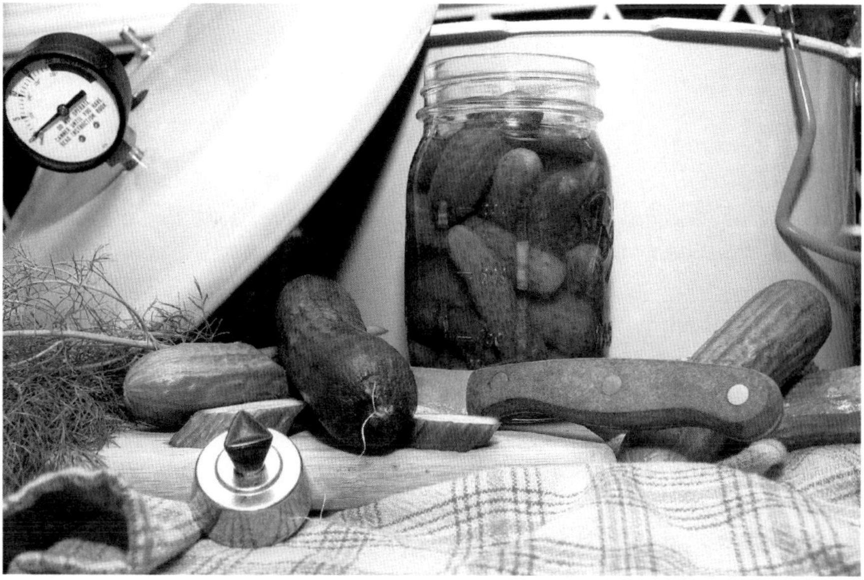

Afterward, before taking the kids home, they'd go to Red Creek to swim. It was their treat for working so hard, but in truth, the dirt that had accumulated on them would never go down the bathtub drain. It was a lot of hard work. For quite a few years, the kids wouldn't eat cucumbers, but Lorraine will tell you, "I always wonder, in looking back on those days, I don't think a person has even lived until they filled a full-size pickup truck with one-inch cucumbers. It was a lot of hard work, but I still treasure the happy memories of our cucumber days in 1975."

The factory had a system. The pickers would be given a number, and the factory supervisors would come out and look at their cucumbers to see if they brought the succulent gherkins or the medium-sized cheap stuff. Sometimes the workers in the pickle factory would be given the larger cucumbers to take home, and their families would have enough to eat until they were sick of them.

The gherkins were the ones you could get the most money for. They were small and savory. One could make money from the medium ones, but you didn't make any more money for the number 3 cucumbers. You didn't want to grow a cucumber larger than a number 3, which would be no more than approximately three inches in length. Many people in the area made their livings by growing and delivering cucumbers to the Wiggins pickle factory, and quite a few of the children in the region worked at the pickle factory after they grew up and finished school. Some folks would work all night long to make a good living. Each community that delivered cucumbers to the pickle factory was part of a rivalry. You had to be careful about mentioning being part of a community that had the best cucumbers.

Rita Restor, a local resident, worked inside the pickle factory, while her father worked in the warehouse where they would ship the pickles out of the factory. Her mother worked there as well, and she cased the jars of pickles at the end of an assembly line. Rita says that her mom had miraculous hands. The pickle jars would come down the line to a big round table. First, she would sit there until you thought she was going to let the jars fall off on the floor. She'd sit there and rest, swing her foot, and then she would get up and take three in each hand and she'd go, Bloop! Bloop! Bloop!

The pickles were jarred as hamburger relish, hotdog relish, hamburger dills, sweet onion pickles, pearl onion relish and the sweet gherkins. According to the people working on establishing the pickle factory museum, it is said that at one time, all the pickles in the world were made at the pickle factory in Wiggins, which was also reputed to be the biggest in the world. Most of the jars were labeled under the brand name Rainbow pickles. The Wiggins pickle factory also had contracts with the government. The factory would stock the labeling machines and put in the different label for whatever company it was doing business with. It packaged for IGA, Rainbow and A&P brands. It had locations in Texarkana, Texas, and New Orleans, Louisiana. When the large semi trucks would come to get the pickles from the factory in Wiggins, they would back up to the factory door loading dock, and they would deliver jarred pickles all over the country. Lorraine's husband drove a pickle truck, and his route took him as far north as North Carolina.

The pickle factory has since shut its doors. Rita is on the pickle factory museum committee, and her committee is working to document its history. There is a lot of history that surrounds the old facility, and the committee has lots of old pictures and relics. When the factory closed, it was broken apart. People bought the old boards and used them to build other facilities. Animals like salt licks, and a man out in the Magnolia community had built different things from the boards, but his cows ate the boards because of the salt.

There is a pecan house that was built in McHenry on Highway 49 of the boards from the Wiggins pickle factory. If the boards had been used to build something out in the woods, the animals would have eaten the boards. Animals loved the taste of the wood from the pickle factory.

There is a rumor that someone's head was found in one of the pickle vats once, and there are rumors about entire pickled people. The vats were humongous, easily the size of a large room. It is rumored that a man working at the Brown & Miller Pickle Factory fell in the pickle vat and stayed there for a while before anyone missed him. No one knows if that story is true. Some say it could have been true because the vats were salted down and the man would have been preserved. It was said that the fellow looked like a pickled mummy when they finally pulled him out. It is said that he lived at Big Level, and his funeral was held at a church called Calvary, which wouldn't open the coffin because of his pickled state. The museum committee has determined that it would have to take the pickle investigation a little further to find out if this story has any validity.

Southerners have a way with cucumbers. Of course, you could just peel and eat the bumpy green delicacies, but you could make a salad with cucumbers in it. You could even make yourself a cucumber sandwich. When you live and work in a community where cucumber is king, you tend to be creative in what you can do with them. Cucumbers can be fried like zucchini and tomatoes. First, coat them with a lightly seasoned cornmeal mixture.

Folks have their own secret ingredients that they add to their favorite recipes, but the basic ingredients in cucumber soup would be to chop or purée two peeled cucumbers and mix with one cup of plain yogurt and one cup of sour cream. Add a cup of chicken broth, salt, pepper, garlic powder and dill to taste. Mix well and chill for at least two hours. On a hot summer day, cold cucumber soup offers a simple treat.

Aside from selling cucumbers to the factory, you could use them to make your own pickles. A mother like Lorraine could even use the cucumbers to create a soothing balm for her tired eyes by slicing and placing ice-cold cucumbers on her eyelids. Well, at least she could hope and dream about such things, and maybe she could find a moment when the kids were all settled in for the night to actually enjoy such relaxation.

Many a southern woman has made a cucumber astringent in her day for a facial cleanse by taking the green delights and putting them in a processor with mint leaves, lemon juice and egg whites, thereby turning them into a purée. Cucumbers are also a simple way to shed water weight because they act as a diuretic.

When you live in rural Mississippi (and most of the state is considered rural), you'll find that folks out in the country have ways to make the best of almost everything. With a glass of iced lemon water, it is yummy. This is the kind of fixings that will take a nation through an economic downturn. Lemon water is a sure delight on a hot summer day, but a pitcher of cucumbers with limes and fresh mint leaves and two cups of sugar will do the trick as well.

The Two-Dollar Mule in Aberdeen

Mr. Douglas H. Strahan grew up in Noxapater, which had one traffic light. Lack of opportunities in the small town made it tough for families during the Great Depression, so Mr. Doug's family drove north to Aberdeen. Times were hard for everyone, and the family became sharecroppers. Sharecroppers shared their crops with the landowners, and they reaped only a very small portion of their labor. In 1935, before the war started, farmers and sharecroppers were farming cotton and peanuts. The government would pay for farmers to grow peanuts. The ground was sandy and favorable for a harvest. The government made oil out of the peanut crop. Most of the poor farmers didn't have any equipment back then. Mr. Doug's family had one plow, and his dad operated it as if he had high-tech equipment. The children weren't allowed to get close to the plow.

There was no money to be spent on "wants" during the Depression, so the custom was to go to town on Saturdays and window-shop. One day, Mr. Doug's dad went to town on Saturday and came back home a little later than his usual time. The sun was going down when the children looked down the road and spotted a figure walking alongside a mule. When they got closer, they realized that it was their old man.

The children had never seen the old man happy or smiling. But as he got close, they saw their father sort of jumping and clicking his heels, and they knew something just wasn't right.

He shouted, "Look what I got for two dollars. A mule! And the owner threw in this horse collar to boot!"

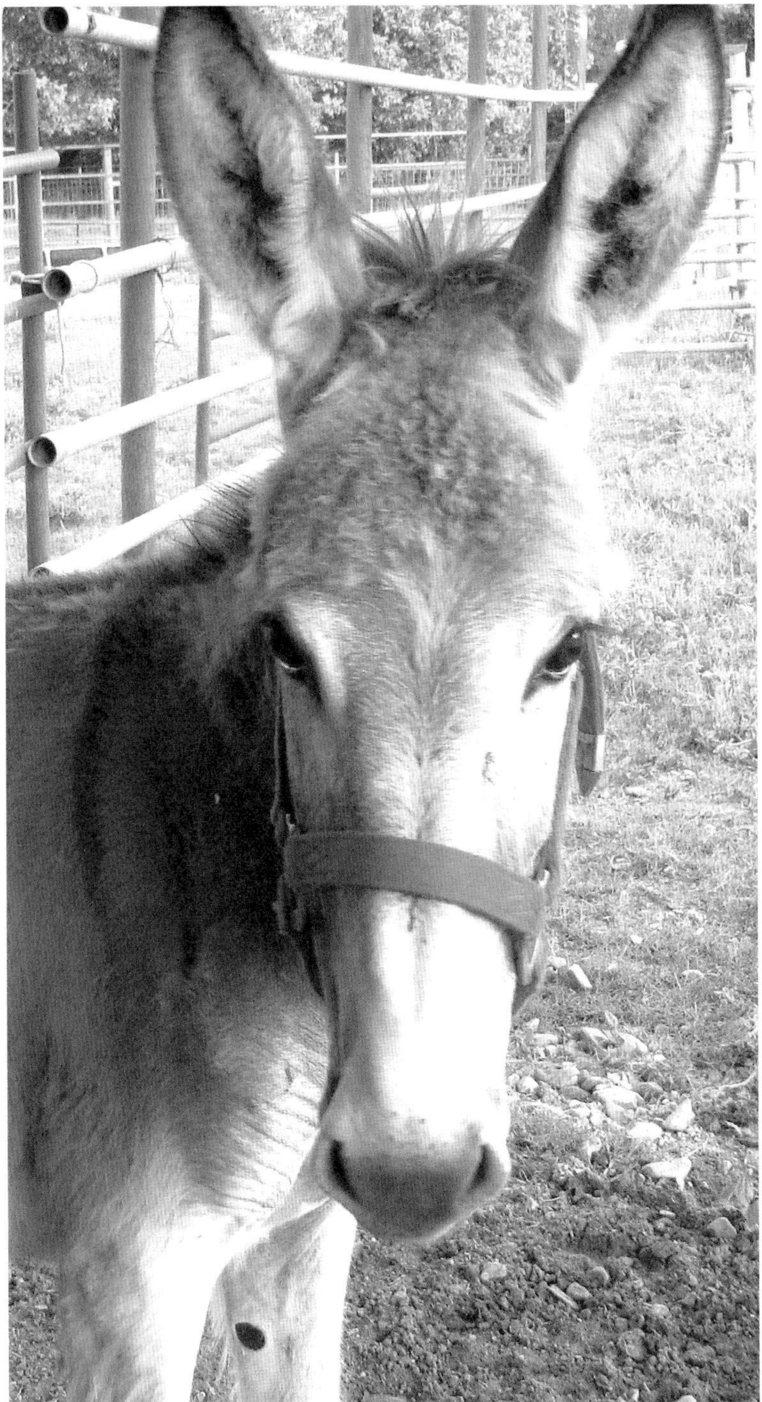

Mr. Doug's father couldn't wait to saddle that mule and get him ready to plow. But his dad wouldn't plow on Sunday. He waited until Monday and took the mule down to the cornfield. That corn would make good fodder. You could stack it and let it dry in the field, and then you could use it for fertilizer and feed for the animals. So when Monday came, they all went down to the cornfield to see this "hotshot" mule in action. To the family's utter amazement, the mule didn't perform. It lay down in the field and started eating and munching on the corn. The old man cussed and screamed and beat it with whatever he could get his hands on, but the mule kept lying on its belly eating corn. The old man didn't know what to do with that mule.

He took it up to the barn and locked it up in the stable. During the night, the mule forced its stable door open and went out into the main area of the barn where the cattle and milk cows were lined up in their stalls. He stumbled upon the fertilizer bin that held the fertilizer chemicals. If anyone, man or animal, dared to eat that stuff, it would kill him for sure, but that mule had itself a feast day. It must have eaten somewhere between twenty-five and fifty pounds of sodium nitrate.

The next day, Mr. Doug's mama went down to the barn early because she was the one who did the milking. The men always said that milking was women's work on the farm, and the men would follow that statement with a hearty, "Amen!" Mama came down around daylight to milk the cows, and to her surprise, the new two-dollar mule was there sitting on its haunches, stiff as a board.

Mama went over to the neighbor's farm and asked to borrow the farmer's metal log chains. Mr. Doug's dad pulled the mule down to the edge of the swamp, unhooked the mule and parked it there.

You can go to Aberdeen and see buzzards circling that spot in the swamp to this very day, and that's the honest truth.

Midwifery in Sandy Hook

Rebecca Pope was Mary Etta Moody's great-great grandmother. She was born sometime between 1840 and 1844, and she died in 1920. It wasn't important to send girls to school back then, so she had only a sixth-grade education. Nobody seemed to care about such things. But she learned to read and write, and she read medical books and learned everything she needed to know about doctoring, and she learned to deliver babies. If anybody was going to have a baby in Sandy Hook, Becky Pope (as she was called) was the one to deliver the infant.

She was very successful. She learned to use bread that had grown mold. We now know that it becomes penicillin when you do certain things to it. Becky Pope also learned how to turn a baby that was about to be born breach.

There was a woman who worked with her called Aunt Glo, short for Glory. Glory was a sixteen-year-old African American child when her mama gave her to Becky so that she, too, could become a midwife. This was after slavery. The child was given to her because her mother knew that Becky made a good living as a midwife. She made a little money, but she often accepted turnip greens, eggs and ham for her wages; you could live, and you could live prosperously on those rations.

One day, Aunt Glo and Becky were going to Old Lady Miller's house. Old Lady Miller had never had a live child, though she had had about four or five miscarriages. She carried some of the babies to full term, but they were born dead.

Mr. Miller called Becky to his house a little farther out past Sandy Hook. Becky and Aunt Glo went down to Mr. Miller's house, and they stayed there two days. Finally, Mrs. Miller went into labor, and Becky and Aunt Glo delivered her a live baby. They left the Millers very, very happy that day.

On their way back to Sandy Hook, they were surprised by a man who jumped out onto the road from behind the bushes. He grabbed the reins of

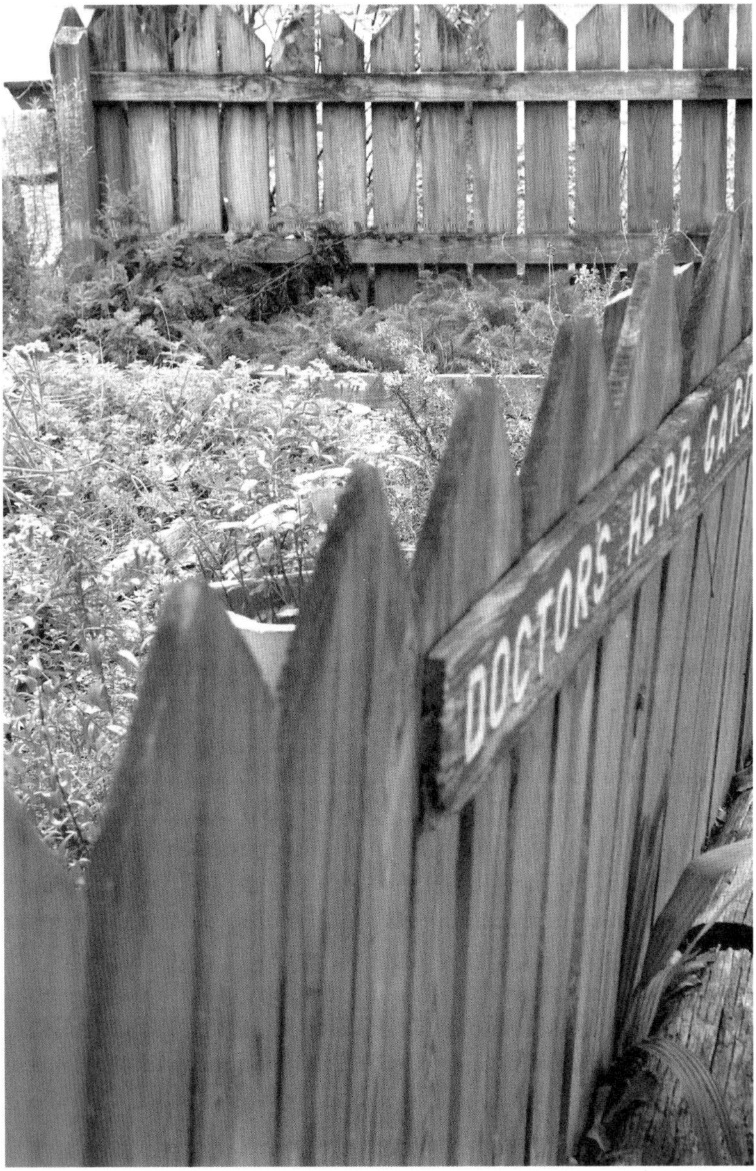

their buggy and made them get out. This was around 1895 or 1900. He got into the buggy and headed toward the Louisiana state line. In the meantime, Aunt Glo and Becky had gone on to Sandy Hook on foot and told the train station clerk that a man had stolen their buggy. There wasn't a phone at the train station, so the clerk telegraphed ahead to the next station using Morse code. It was around 1:00 p.m., and would you believe the sheriff had the thief in custody and got the buggy back before dark? The thief was tried and sent to Parchman Prison.

Throughout the course of their lives, delivering babies is all that Becky and Aunt Glo ever did. These were two women whose life circumstances afforded them little hope. But they learned to be midwives, and as such, they became fairly successful. Aunt Glo was just as good as Becky when it came to delivering babies.

Becky had ten children of her own. Aunt Glo had only four because her husband, a Pullman porter, had been hit by lightning and died at the age of thirty-four. Aunt Glo's children were well educated. The eldest son went to Howard University, and Becky's children all went to school in Mississippi or Louisiana.

Becky lost only one pregnant mother, and that was because the woman went into labor on a train. By the time the train arrived in Sandy Hook and the conductor stopped to get the woman off, she had been in labor well over the normal time for delivery, and there was nothing Becky or Aunt Glo could do to save her.

Becky and Aunt Glo were old when they quit delivering babies. It almost killed Becky when Aunt Glo died. They had been very close and had worked together for many years.

The John Ford House of Sandy Hook

In Sandy Hook, there is a house called the Ford House. It was built sometime around the turn of the nineteenth century. Some accounts say the house was built sometime between 1805 and 1810, and it is still standing today. Mary Etta Moody tells the story of the Ford House, and she's certainly qualified to do so. She is a direct descendant of Reverend John Ford. Reverend Ford was the first Methodist circuit rider in the area.

This is the same house where Andrew Jackson had spent some time when he became ill while traveling to Louisiana for the Battle of New Orleans. One of Reverend Ford's sons went to New Orleans with Jackson and was killed in the battle. Andrew Jackson played a major role in this memorable American victory. He was one of the commanders and leaders during the battle that started on January 8, 1815. It was the last major battle of the War of 1812. The battle is considered to be one of the greatest American land victories of the war. It is said that at the end of the battle, General Jackson personally went to the convent to thank the nuns for praying. Even though the odds were against the American soldiers and in favor of the British, Jackson managed to establish himself as a national military hero.

Prior to making his mark during war times, President Andrew Jackson killed a man who accused him of cheating on a horse race bet and then insulted his wife, Rachel. Throughout his life, Jackson established himself as a colorful character. This is a much different personae than one would assume to be characteristic of a president of our great country. Jackson married a woman who wasn't quite divorced from her first husband. Actually, she did not realize that her first husband had not finalized their divorce. But the scandal seemed to follow her everywhere. Andrew loved her, and they often would travel throughout Mississippi along the Natchez Trace, journeying from Nashville, Tennessee, to Natchez. Rachel was a colorful, raven-haired beauty who would learn the dances of Tennessee and bring them back to her friends in Mississippi.

Jackson was known to be argumentative and physically violent and had no problem dueling to resolve an issue. He killed Charles Dickinson in a duel but only after being shot himself. It is said that a bullet pierced Jackson's chest a few inches below his heart and that the blood dripped into his boots, but he stood firm, stayed his hand and shot and killed Dickinson. Jackson suffered the rest of his life from pain that resulted from his wound.

Jackson was known as a man of contradictions and of scandal. Although he promoted himself as a man of the people, many people hated him. John Ford knew all about Jackson's reputation, and under no circumstances would he allow his house to be defamed with the likes of Andrew Jackson. Suffice it to say, Andrew Jackson was a brawler and a gambler, and he traded slaves and horses. He was known as Old Hickory because he was quick-tempered and welcomed a good fight.

There was an occasion when Andrew Jackson was sick and was offered the opportunity to stay at the Ford House. Ford told him, "I will offer you the hospitality of my house, but you will have to promise me one thing."

Andrew Jackson asked, "What is that?"

Ford responded, "Son, I understand that you use vulgar language. You will not utter any vulgar language in my home, and you will come to vespers for prayers every evening. If you agree, then yes, you can have the hospitality of staying in my home."

Jackson was not allowed to drink in the Ford House, either. Since Andrew Jackson's vocabulary was filled with colorful language, this would be the first time that he ever remained quiet for any length of time. But he was also very ill, so whether he was driven to silence due to his health or in fear that he might curse in the Reverend John Ford's home is not clear. His bed is still in the house.

If you happen to go to the Columbia courthouse to read John Ford's will, you will find out that he had a copper screw (copper tubing for a whiskey still) that he bequeathed to his middle son. There are some who considered moonshine a prescription for medicinal purposes. John Ford was very religious. In fact, he was a stickler with regard to religion, so there is no way that he would use moonshine for anything other than making medicine.

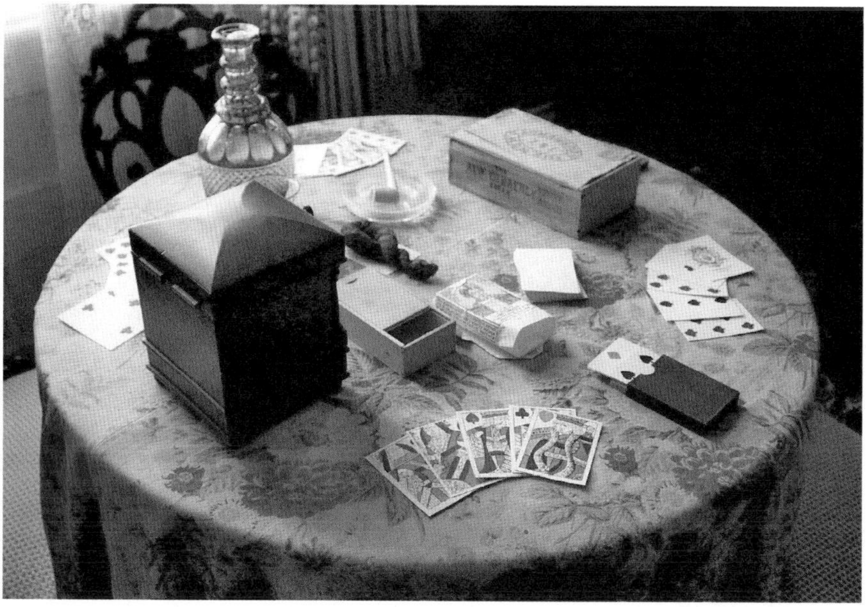

It has been said that Reverend Ford had hundreds of acres of land in both Louisiana and Mississippi, but he settled his homestead in Mississippi because there was a code in Louisiana, the Code Noir, which said that slaves were not allowed to read or write. It was Reverend Ford's belief that his slaves should be able to read so that God's word from the Bible would be part of their daily lives. His slaves were required to attend his church services, and as was the custom, they had to sit in the balcony. It is a well-known fact that the bricks on the lower part of the Ford House were fashioned by those very same slaves. When John Ford freed his slaves, they wanted to take on his name as their last name. But it was the reverend's desire that they take on the name of St. Peter. Therefore, the descendants of John Ford's slaves today are known as Peters. Every one of Reverend Ford's slaves was named in his will.

During the Civil War, the Union army had come into that area looking for a particular Native American who knew how to get into New Orleans without crossing Lake Pontchartrain by boat and without getting one's feet wet. This could prove to be a profitable strategy for the army. Somehow the word got back to the Native American that he was of interest to the Union army, and he hid inside the Ford House in hopes of deceiving the soldiers. Catherine R. Ford, John Ford's wife, was very old at this time, and John had already died.

The Union army never did find the man. They searched the entire house, never finding the Native American, who was right behind the wall behind the bed where Catherine R. Ford lay. Essentially, she was dying. Later, after the Union army left, the Indian outfitted and went back into the woods and was never seen again.

The first Methodist conference was held in the Ford House. Many generations of people lived there. A family by the name of Rankin was the last family to live in the home, which now belongs to the Marion County Historical Society.

Keep Okolona Hummin'

The pride of a community comes from knowing its history.
—Anonymous

The town of Okolona has its own song, created years ago and sung to the tune of "She'll Be Coming Round the Mountain."

"Keep Okolona Hummin'"

Okolona came around the mountain when he came,
He was puffing away at his peace pipe when he came,
Later he rode the GM&O and he watched the soybeans grow,
And he plowed the cotton fields row by row.

Here we are in Okolona….3,000 [folks] *or more,*
And we love this little town we did explore,
Though our problems may be many,
Very soon we won't have any
And we'll all be as happy as before.

We will stand together brothers black and white,
To develop a better spirit outright,

To expand our recreation and excel as part of the nation
And create a better atmosphere of love.

The town of Okolona is named after a Chickasaw Indian chief. He was known to be one of the handsomest men around. In fact, folks would say that he was "a fine-looking specimen of a man."

At one time, the town of Okolona was larger than Tupelo, even though it is only 6.4 square miles. It is a small town with an outlying community that has connected with it over the years. Okolona was the center of transportation years ago. The community has approximately 250 historic properties. Fewer than three thousand people live in the town now, but there has been a lot of vibrant activity taking place in Okolona over the years.

Okolona was a railroad town that served as a terminal point between Mobile, Alabama, and Nashville, Tennessee. The railroad gangs were headquartered in Okolona, and you could hear the gandy dancers' chant and the methodical shuffle of the men who worked to line the railroad tracks. There is nothing that can compare to that sound! It has virtually disappeared from our country's history. But if you look really hard, you just might find a "section" gang member still alive today.

During the Depression, Okolona was one of the hardest-hit cities in the United States. Even still, it was stylish for men to wear hats and caps, and the women wore large hats when they went into town. During the '30s and '40s, there were only a few hotels in Okolona, but even these are long gone now. A lot of families would have rooms in their houses that they would "let" (rent), and most of the time the railroad men would stay there.

The community doctor would blow a whistle so that folks would know he was on his way to someone's house. Okolona is also known for having a Confederate hospital and cemetery.

There is a place outside of Okolona called Hell's Half-Acre. It later became known as Paradise Valley. That's where the corn whiskey was made years ago. A kettle was found in a pool, and that's the kettle that was used to make the whiskey. It was not an easy task to catch moonshiners in the act, even though their stills were usually located close to nearby waterways. Each moonshiner had a devoted customer base. Their work was risky business that made some people nervous. It is said that the revenuers were afraid to go to Hell's Half-Acre lest they be killed by the fearless moonshiners who worked deep out in the woods and were armed to the teeth.

During the 1930s, it is said that a hermit by the name of McCauley lived in an old well at the end of Main Street that was fashioned as a cave/cavern

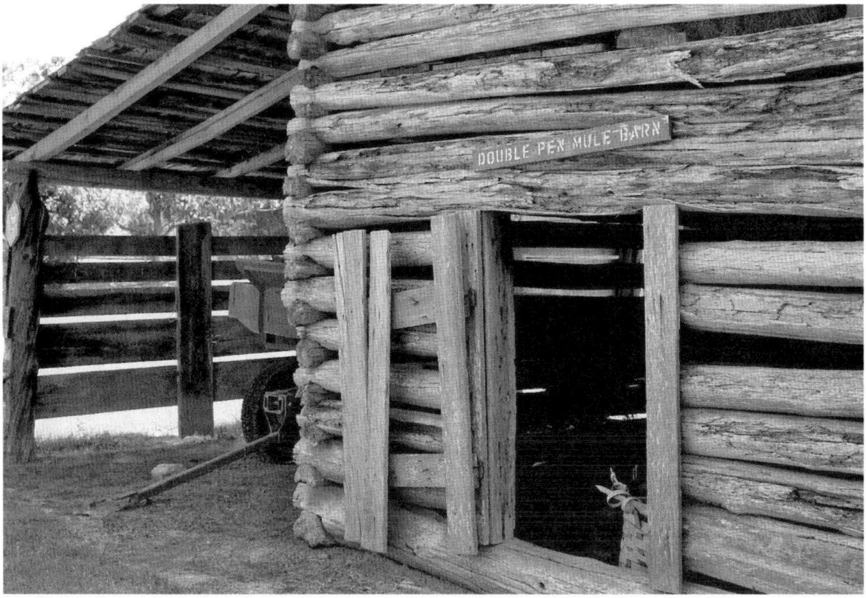

underneath the ground. He was a tall white man with a big mustache. He dug three rooms in the lime rock underground, and he covered the ceiling with tin. It was a really nice cave. He used a ladder to get in and out, and he even had a little hole for smoke to escape. Aboveground, he had a garden. He even had a few cattle (cows and sheep). His son, Daniel McCauley, lived in Shannon, Mississippi. It is alleged that he ran with the Jesse James gang. An article from the *Tupelo Journal* verifies that Jesse James was known to frequent the area around Tupelo. Some say the McCauleys may have been kin to Jesse James, but others say that he never met them at all.

A horse trader who owned a mule barn nearby took McCauley under his wing. Folks would ride their bikes past the well at top speed because they were afraid. When McCauley died, it was a while before anyone missed him. He is buried in the cemetery in Okolona next to his son.

Okolona used to host foot parties or toe parties in the schoolhouses. Girls would hide behind the window curtains, and the fellows would pick the girls they wanted to dance with by looking at their feet poking out from behind the bottom of the curtain fabric. There would be live guitar, banjo and fiddle music. Someone would even play a one-string tub. Once the accordion and washboard joined in, the excitement was the next item on the agenda.

The Pulitzer Prize–winning syndicated American public affairs columnist William Raspberry was born and raised in Okolona.

Love Is Like Cornbread

A Story of Unconditional Love in Columbia

Down in South Mississippi in Columbia during the early 1900s, there lived a man named Chalmus who stood eight feet tall. He was lanky, and when he walked, he commanded a certain respect. He was a family man and had two daughters and a wife whom he called "Mama."

Now, Mama loved to cook. She would go into the kitchen, and she would cook all kinds of things, but folks especially liked her cornbread. She would put buttermilk in her cornbread and a little shortening, but she would cut back on that shortening and add a big scoop of mayonnaise. It made the cornbread taste like a piece of cake. Her girls said that her cornbread tasted like a little bit of heaven. Mama never ate any of her own cornbread, however. She thought to herself, "If I taste one bite and it doesn't taste like heaven, I'll know those girls were teasing me."

She would fix Chalmus a plate of food, and a lot of times he wouldn't come home in time for dinner because he would be out in the woods back behind the house hunting. That was his domain. If he didn't come home for dinner, Mama would wrap his plate and carry it out to the tree stump at the edge of the woods and leave it there for him.

Now, Chalmus would hunt for rabbit, possum and squirrel. One day, he came home with a fever and took to the bed. Mama didn't know what was wrong with him, but after a few days, she called on the doctor. He came, but he couldn't figure out what was wrong with Chalmus, so he just told Mama to give him something to drink and, if he started feeling a little bit better, to try and get him to eat something—especially some of her cornbread. If he took a bite of her cornbread, she would know that he was feeling much better.

Since the doctor couldn't figure out what was wrong with Chalmus, Mama called on Miss Mamie, the community herbalist, who fixed him a concoction. Mama gave it to Chalmus, but it didn't do him any good.

The next day, he got up out of the bed and walked right out of the house and went straight to the woods, and he didn't come back for a long, long time. A year passed before folks started talking about him, wondering what he was doing out in the woods. The gossip spread like wildfire. They started calling him a wild woodsman. As a matter of fact, there were two boys, six and seven years old apiece, who double-dared each other to go out into the woods. Well, they walked out there, and they ran right into Chalmus. That eight-foot-tall man looked down on those boys with a tree limb in his hand. It frightened those boys. The eldest boy ran "boogety-boogety-boogety" back to Columbia, and the youngest one fell faint on the ground. When he came to, he was too afraid to open his eyes. The first thing he noticed was someone singing: "Amazing grace, how sweet the sound…" The boy didn't realize who was singing. As he came to, he felt himself in the arms of Chalmus. He opened his eyes and realized that Chalmus's voice was the sweetest voice he had ever heard. He may have simply been glad to be alive. The young boy looked around, and on the ground, he saw a dog and the tree limb that Chalmus had in his hand before the boy fainted. That wild woodsman must have used that limb to hit that dog. That was the dog that the folks in town said had rabies. Chalmus had just saved that boy's life. The young boy thanked him and went back to town, but the eldest boy had beat him there and told everyone about "the crazy man out in the woods." The younger boy tried to set the record straight and tried to let everybody know that Chalmus was just trying to save their lives. But the boy couldn't convince the people, no matter how hard he tried. The people wanted to continue talking about Chalmus. They wanted to believe what they wanted to believe. Gossip somehow has a much sweeter taste on the lips and tongue.

It was two years before Chalmus came back home. He walked into the house just as suddenly as he had left. He didn't even know that he had been gone for so long, but he was glad to see his family. He picked up his girls and held them in his arms. They felt like little princesses sitting on top of the world. He would hold them in the crux of his arms until they grew to be twelve years old. They were big girls, but Chalmus was a big man.

Well, not long after that, he took to drinking. Chalmus would go down into the town of Columbia, drunk as a skunk. He would teeter and totter around, and he would frighten the people. They had to call on Sheriff Strickler.

The sheriff walked over to Chalmus and said, "I'm going to have to take you on home."

He reached upward with his hand toward Chalmus's hand, and Chalmus reached down with his long, lanky arm. The sheriff was only five foot eight.

Chalmus took Sheriff Strickler's hand, and he said, "Okay, Little Strickler, I'se ready to go."

Chalmus called everyone "little" something or other. The sheriff took him on home. Not long after that, Chalmus stopped drinking. He told Mama that he wanted to go to church with her, but he was afraid that the folks down at the church would talk about him and call him a drinking man. He just didn't know what he should really do.

With a chuckle on her lips, Mama said, "Whenever you're ready, you just come on."

When Chalmus felt the time was right, he got up on a bright Sunday morning, looked out the window and saw the sun coming up over the horizon. It was time for him to go to church. But he took so long getting ready. Mama had got all the cooking done, and she stood in the doorway looking at him.

"When you're ready to come, Chalmus, just come on over to the church house. I'm going on. I don't want to be late."

She walked out the door. Chalmus continued taking his time. He went to the closet and picked out the brown suit that had to be ordered and especially made for him. He dusted it off, put it on and looked in the mirror for a while.

By this time, Mama was already at the church house. The service had started. She anxiously looked back, but she didn't see Chalmus. The preacher started preaching. She looked back once again, but he wasn't there. When the preacher "opened the doors of the church" (a saying used in traditional black churches to indicate that if someone wanted to come forward and join the church, this was their time to stand, come forward, make a profession of faith and join), Mama was hoping that Chalmus would walk in the doors of the church ready to accept the Lord, but she looked back and he still had not arrived.

The church service ended, and it was time to meet, greet and share fellowship on the church grounds outside before going home. Chalmus wasn't coming to church that day. Miss Mamie told Mama that she had a good piece of righteous gossip to share with her. So Mama told the girls to go on home along the normal route, and she would meet them at the house.

Mama was going to walk along the road that Miss Mamie traveled and then cut across to her house. The girls skipped on down the road laughing and singing songs to one another. Somehow Mama made it to the house before they did. Papa wasn't there. She picked up his plate, wrapped it in some newspaper and took it out to the tree stump and went back into the house to piddle around.

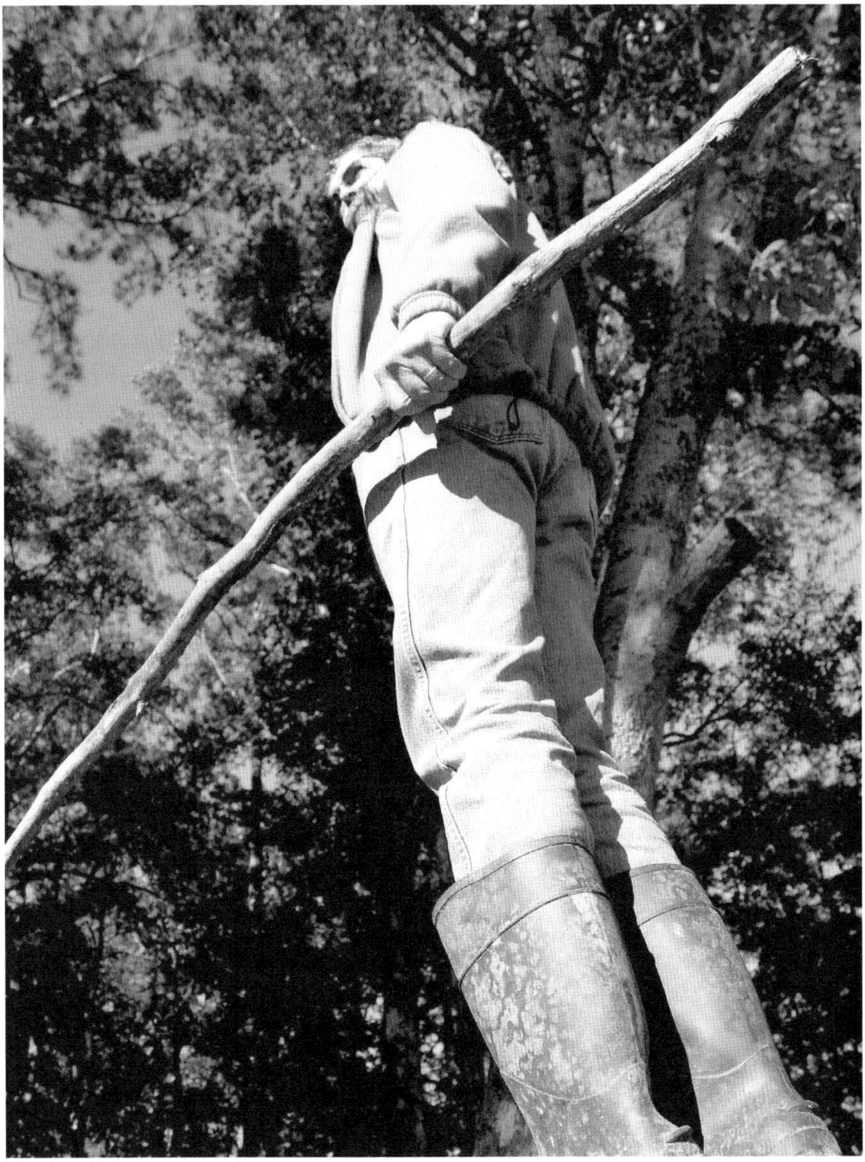

Suddenly, she heard the girls' piercing cries, "Mama! Mama! Mama!"

They came running into the house terrified.

"Mama, we were walking out along the edge of the woods and we saw something that looked like a big old tree trunk lying on the ground. But Mama, it was Papa! Papa is dead! Papa is dead!"

With each word that poured from her lips, Mama patted the back of her hand into the palm of her other hand as she said, "Girls, go out to town and tell the man at the funeral parlor to come and get Papa's body."

The girls did as they were told. Mama stepped out of the house and walked over to the edge of the woods and picked up Papa's plate and brought it back into the house. She laid it on the table, unwrapped it and picked up the cornbread and took one bite. When she did, she realized that her cornbread did taste like a little bit of heaven—just like her marriage to Papa. She had loved him unconditionally.

She stood there reminiscing, thinking about their lives together and about that time he stayed out in the woods for two years. She was still thinking when the man from the funeral parlor walked up the steps and knocked on the screen door.

Peering inside, he said, "I've loaded Chalmus's body onto the back of my truck. You know what I'm going to have to do, don't you? I'll have to order his casket from New Orleans because it will have to be specially made."

Mama said, "I know," and invited him inside.

"Can I offer you something to eat?" she said with a glint in her eye (because she knew her cooking was something special).

He nodded his head and said, "I'd like to take the plate with me, and I promise to bring it back."

Mama wrapped up his plate, but he unwrapped it as soon as she put it in his hand. He took one bite of her cornbread and said, "Mmm! Mmm! Mmm! Your cornbread tastes like a little bit of heaven!"

The Corinth Railroad Story

All that's left of Philmore is his guitar. There was a time when folks used to come out of the temporary shelters of the tent city, and they would sit down around the old oak trees. Kids and grown folks alike loved to hear what Philmore had to say. They could see him clear as day. He would sit there and point to the grove of trees. That's the way he always started the stories.

He would point and say, "Right over there. That's where it all started here in Corinth."

Philmore was the head man in the railroad camps in Corinth in the mid-1800s. The railroad was going to connect Corinth with Hamburg, a point along the Tennessee River. You see, Mississippi ranked among the first five rail systems to be built in the United States. The second was built in Woodville, Mississippi, in 1838 on Judge McGeehee's plantation.

Philmore was proud to be part of the action. This was the beginning of the iron highways across America. It offered the hope of freedom, but Philmore didn't think so at first.

He remembered one Friday that he was going to quit working on the railroads. He told the other workers that he would hide if he had to, but he wasn't going back. The work was too hard.

He stayed out in the woods all weekend carousing like a hound dog until his friends came to him with a warning. "Don't you spit in the well from which you may want to drink one day," they said. "If you get caught out here, we are going to have to use our shovels to dig your grave."

Next work day, Philmore was back on the job, and he was still telling stories. Philmore told a story about Heddy to get everyone's attention. He told about the time Heddy wanted to die. She wanted slavery to end so badly that she was going to end it for herself.

She laid down on that railroad track, and he went to pointing and said, "Right over there."

He saw it with his own eyes. Heddy was childlike, and those times were too hard. Slavery wasn't going to end for at least fourteen more years. The blacks on the plantation labored even harder picking cotton once the railroad was built, but the work was just too hard. It was a tough job, but it was a race to connect the East and West Coasts to the North and South for trade. You see, in Mississippi, the train toted cotton up the Mississippi River to Memphis.

Every evening when Heddy came home from picking cotton, she said, "I smells like dirt. I don't want to live no more. From dust I came, and to dust I will return. The Lord don't care!"

Everyone told her, "The Lord do care! That's why those who are alive are alive."

Philmore said that when he found Heddy laying on the railroad tracks, he snatched her up. He must have stared at her for a whole five minutes before he said anything. When he did, he said, "Chile, you ain't doing nothing but mixing up homemade sin!"

Heddy got scared that lightning was going to strike her dead. She had done some things wrong in her time, but mixing up homemade sin was devil's work, and she didn't want no part in that. Heddy didn't go back to the railroad tracks for a long time.

Finally, she forgot about that time. She forgot because Philmore would sit her down with the rest of the folks, and he'd tell her stories right along with the rest of them. He told her about the time her mama snuck down to the grove of trees and watched the gandy dancers work their rhythm keeping time so that the men could get the job done. First the surveyor checked out the land. He had to make sure no Indians impeded their progress. After that, the graders made sure that everything was smooth. And after that, some of the men laid down the crossties, and then the rails were laid. They were laying bridge rails back then. Next the iron spike was placed and hammered in. A dozen men laid at least two miles of track a day. This was going on all across America from the late 1700s to the mid-1800s. They say that a man died for every mile of track that was laid, either killed by the fierce nature of the wilds, the hazards of construction or God knows what. It took a tough and rugged man to help build the railroad tracks. Work gangs suffered from the effects of floods, the bubonic plague, anthrax, extreme cold, cholera, landslides and bandits.

Most of the time, these were drinking men. At night, they would drink and they kept up enough of a stink to hair-lip hell, and they would still be skunked the next day. It seemed that there was much that they wanted to forget.

It is said that a golden spike was driven into the last crosstie in Utah by a nameless laborer. Actually, it wasn't hammered in: it was dropped

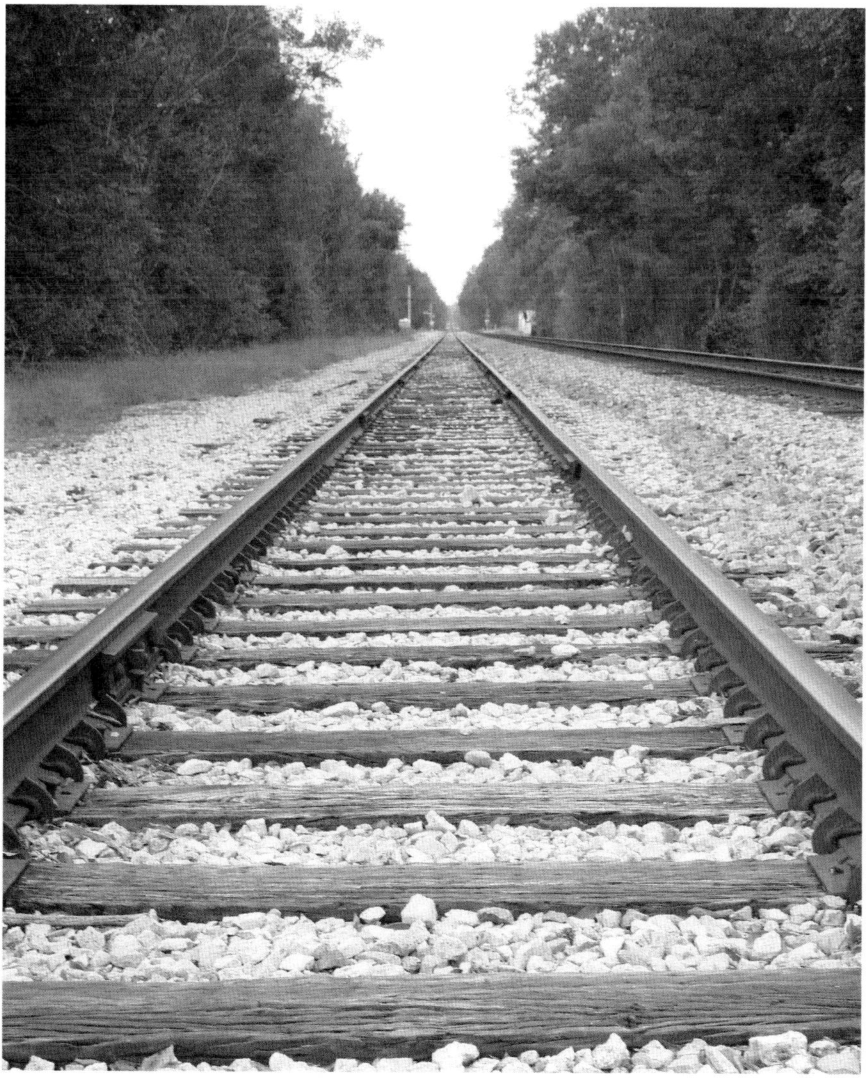

into a pre-drilled hole. Also, it wasn't a golden spike. It was an iron spike, but storytellers have told the golden-spike version of this story for years. Thomas Durant, president of the Union Pacific Railroad, was supposed to have placed that last spike, but he was too unsteady after a night of drinking to even make an attempt.

Anyway, Heddy's mama watched the men as they worked. She heard the railroad songs, and she saw their peculiar shuffle. There was a methodical harmony and rhythm to what they did, a lining rhythm of sorts. She walked back home dancing a jig. She danced that dance every day, and then she got an idea that would liven up that railroad camp. No one had ever seen her dance that jig, so she decided to hold a contest. Philmore remembered it with the juice-joy of laughter. She said that if anyone could guess how she did her dance, they would win a prize. Folks were more honest back then. Heddy's mama would let them know with certainty if they had won, and the prize would be two peach cobblers. Everyone in that camp tried out. One of the women almost guessed the dance. She rocked left/right, left/right, eight times. But then she messed up on the rest of the dance.

One of the fellas tried out, and he almost guessed the dance. He rocked back and forth eight times, pushing both arms double-time from side to side: left/left, right/right, but he didn't know how to end the dance. It seemed that no one could guess, and finally it was time to go. Everyone went back to their makeshift homes. Heddy's mama went to her tent, and she danced the dance one more time so that she wouldn't forget. But Philmore saw her shadow dancing by the light in her tent. Philmore learned how to do that dance that night, but he didn't want Heddy's mama to know that he had seen her.

The next day, he went to his best friend and asked him to do the dance at the next contest. Philmore's friend was a very large man, but he was a very good friend. He didn't know how to dance and didn't think he was agile enough to carry out the steps. Philmore taught him the dance, and he danced at the next contest and won. Philmore's friend was so large that it was hard to tell if he was doing the dance right. But he won nonetheless and won those two peach cobblers.

Philmore and his friend celebrated out in the woods. They danced and celebrated, and while they danced in a circle, those pies disappeared. Philmore never could explain that one. But from that day until this one, folks would gather under that tree to hear stories. The time would always end with the story of the gandy dance, the dance that mimicked the hard work of the men who built the rail system in Corinth, Mississippi. Unless a person was ailing, when Philmore finished storytelling, everyone jumped up, and the fun began. Philmore would sing the gandy dancer's song while everyone danced, and the folks couldn't wait until the next time Philmore told stories.

When I get in Illinois, I'm going to spread the news about the Florida boys
Shove it over—Hey! Hey! Can you line it? Ha ha!
Clack-a-lacka-lacka-lacka-lacka-lacka

A nickel's worth of bacon and a dime's worth of lard
I could buy more, but the times too hard!
Shove it over—Hey! Hey! Can you line it? Ha ha!
Clack-a-lacka-lacka-lacka-lacka-lacka

Tell you what the hobo told the bum, if you get any cornbread save me some!
Shove it over—Hey! Hey! Can you line it? Ha ha!
Clack-a-lacka-lacka-lacka-lacka-lacka

I asked my captain for the time of day, he got mad and threw his watch away!
Shove it over—Hey! Hey! Can you line it? Ha ha!
Clack-a-lacka-lacka-lacka-lacka-lacka

Captain can't read and the captain can't write, how do he know that the time is right!
Shove it over—Hey! Hey! Can you line it? Ha ha!
Clack-a-lacka-lacka-lacka-lacka-lacka

Saw a woman walking across the field, her mouth exhausting like an automobile!
Shove it over—Hey! Hey! Can you line it? Ha ha!
Clack-a-lacka-lacka-lacka-lacka-lacka

Clack-a-lacka-lacka-lacka-lacka-lacka

Natchez: Back in the Day

In 2016, the city of Natchez will commemorate its tricentennial by reflecting on its three hundred years of existence. The city is older than these United States. However, the focus of the community's history has been influenced by more recent recollections, even though its history dates back prior to the Civil War.

African Americans have accomplished a great deal. The first man of color to hold any official office in the state of Mississippi was John Roy Lynch, who served not only as justice of the peace but also as postmaster immediately following the war. He would go on within one year's time to become a member of the first integrated session of the Mississippi legislature, where he fought for civil rights and public education. Ultimately, he became speaker of the House, the only man of color in the history of the state, to this day, to hold that esteemed office.

Hiram Rhodes Revels, who led the pulpit of the Zion Chapel AME Church in Natchez, went on to become the first man of color to serve in either house of the U.S. Congress, as he was the nation's first black U.S. senator. There were five cities throughout the former states of the Confederacy that elected black mayors during that period of Reconstruction. Natchez was one of those five cities and the only one in the state of Mississippi. There was a growing black community in Natchez that was becoming self-sustaining in business. Southern whites wanted to regain control. They wanted to redeem the white man in the South and put in place laws and provisions that would hinder black participation in the electoral process and economic

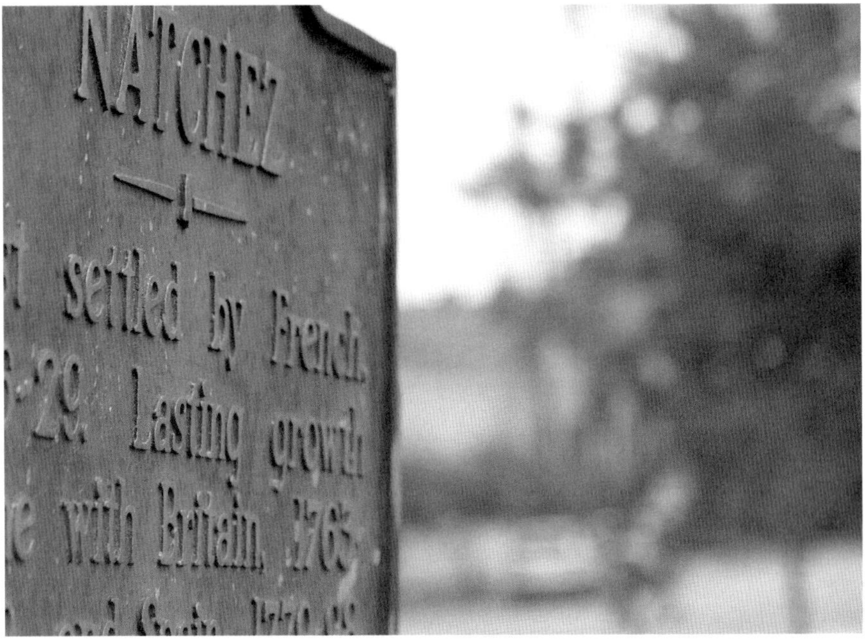

development. Some of the rights taken away by these laws and provisions would not be restored until the passage of the Voting Rights Act in 1965. So from 1890 to 1965, blacks were systemically and illegally locked out of participation in government because they were restricted from voting.

Natchez was not specifically a large-scale farming community. In its early days, it was home to some of the wealthiest individuals in this country. There were more millionaires in Natchez per capita than any other city of its size in the nation because it was ground zero for what had become the nation's number-one cash crop and moneymaker: King Cotton. Natchez was the location of the town homes of those wealthy plantation owners. It was not the site of the working plantations, but it was the site of the marketplace where those business deals transpired.

You have to take into account that prior to the Louisiana Purchase in 1803, Natchez was the southwestern border to the U.S. territory. The nation's landholdings extended only to the Atlantic Ocean, west to the Mississippi and to parts north coming downriver as far as Natchez. If you would have gone

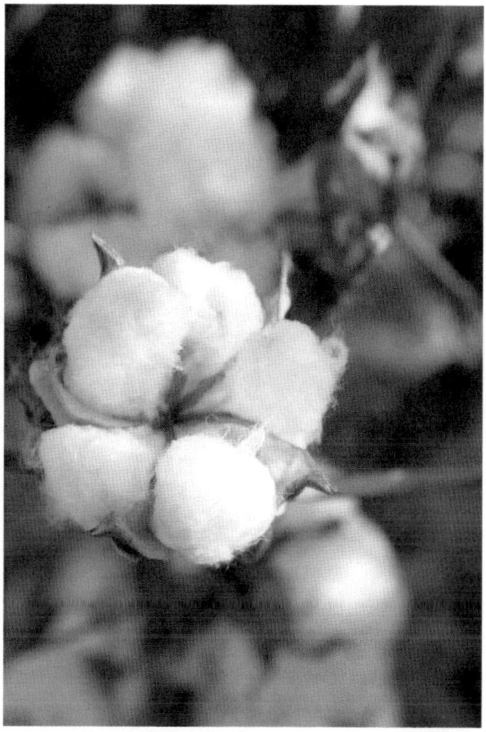

west of Natchez back then, you would have found yourself in a different country: French-controlled Louisiana. Natchez was the end of the line along what was then the nation's superhighway. The highest concentration of enslaved people anywhere throughout this nation was in the Mississippi region as they worked with King Cotton and, later, Queen Sugar in Louisiana.

"Forks of the Road" was not specifically a slave auction site. In today's times, it would be comparable to Walmart. Slave traffickers would import enslaved people from various parts of the country, with many of them coming primarily from the Virginia area. At Forks of the Road, people could order the type of enslaved person that they wanted to purchase. One wouldn't necessarily bid in an auction, but customers would go shopping for specific needs, such as a cook or a field hand. If the type of enslaved person needed was not available, the salesperson would indicate when he would have that type of commodity. It could be compared to today's automotive dealerships because many people during those times could not afford to pay cash. That is why there was no auction. At Forks of the Road, credit deals would be made, and if you didn't pay, the seller could repossess the commodity.

In addition to Forks of the Road, there was another place in the town of Natchez where people of different social classes met called "Under the Hill." The city of Natchez sits two hundred feet above the water line at the river. It is one of the highest points along the entire length of the Mississippi River,

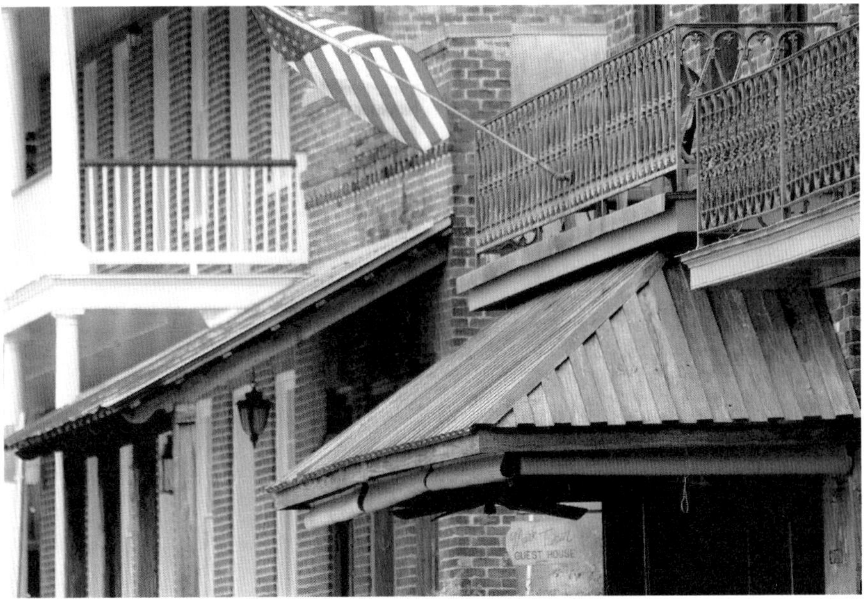

and the area along that side of the town got the name "Under the Hill" because Natchez sat on a hilltop. The area at one time had the character and culture that one would associate with any maritime or dock area. The site was considered to be a rogue gentleman's paradise. There were opportunities for businesses. There was also gambling, drinking and more than just a few loose women visiting or plying their wares in that area. In fact, some have said that it was so wild in that area that it would take an event of biblical proportions to straighten things out. The U.S. Army Corps of Engineers made changes to the flow of the river farther north to improve steamboat navigation between the years 1837 and 1848. Because of those changes, rapid waters from the Mississippi came and wiped out one street that used to be part of a bustling area in the community. Natchez was only Under the Hill from the 1710s to the late 1790s, when the city was laid out in squares during the Spanish occupation. Some of the early homes from that period still exist.

They say the boll weevil was brought to America in the doll baby of a little girl. This tale corresponds with the true story of Walter Burling, a Natchez-area planter who went to Mexico City in 1806 on official U.S. business.

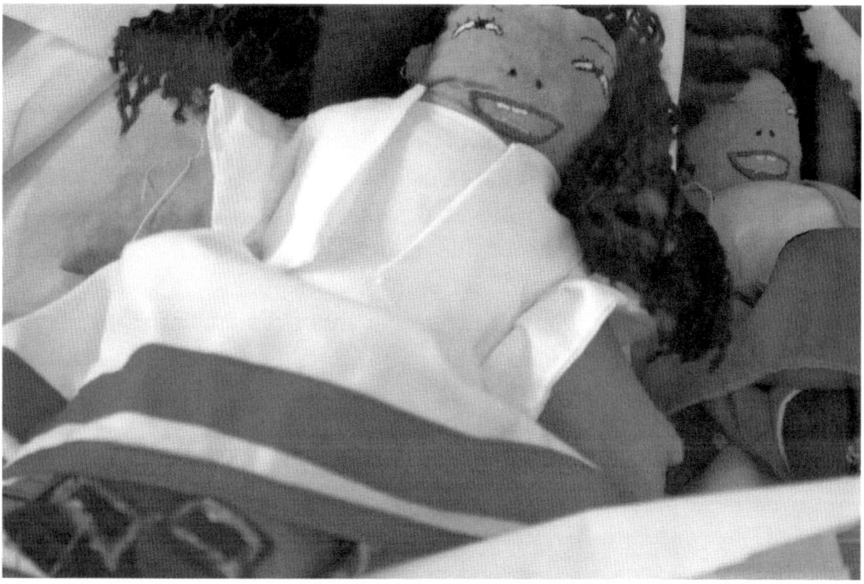

During this trip, he confiscated cottonseeds, which he then brought into the United States. He was able to bring the cottonseeds into America by hiding them inside doll babies that he then shipped by boat to Natchez. This cottonseed was a major contributor in the production of a higher-quality cottonseed across the South.

The Natchez Museum of African American History and Culture has dolls on display that show how the cottonseeds were used as stuffing inside of dolls in order to transport them into the Natchez area. It was those seeds that were cross-pollinated with domestic strands, which developed and became the most profitable and highest-quality cotton the world had known at that time, even more so than the Egyptian cotton. While the story about a little girl traveling with a baby doll stuffed with boll weevils and cottonseeds is just a folktale, there is no doubt that Walter Burling helped the insect migrate to the South.

One of the individuals involved with the development of a new strand of cotton was Rushworth Nutt, from Rodney, a few miles north of Natchez. His son, Haller, was the owner of the House of Longwood. He was one of the wealthy planters whose home is still one of the crown jewels of the antebellum structures in the city of Natchez. As construction was being undertaken on the home, notification came that the war had started. Haller had contracted with Samuel Sloan, a Philadelphia architect. Together they designed the plan for what is called an antebellum "Oriental villa." Most of the constructed homes always had four sides to them, but Haller and Samuel decided that they would build an octagonal house named Longwood in 1859. Longwood, also known as Nutt's Folly, happens to be the largest of the octagonal homes in the nation. The thought of building the house with an onion-shaped dome in Mississippi was highly controversial, and it was a major undertaking.

When word came that war had broken out, some of the northern artisans who had come to Natchez with Samuel Sloan to work as the supervisors or foremen on the project realized that they were Philadelphia Yankees in the Deep South. They dropped their tools and everything they were working with in the middle of the floor and high-tailed it out of town to make their way back up north. Samuel's story states that they all felt the conflict would be short-term, so they figured they would leave everything right there because the workers would be back. However, the war went on for five years. During that same period of time, Haller Nutt became very ill and died before the war ended. Construction on the house was never completed. One of the things that Haller and Sloan managed to do was to finish the basement, and the Nutt family lived in the basement of the home from the 1860s until approximately 1968.

Basements were not common in the South. Usually, the foundations of houses were aboveground, but this one was built on a hill for ventilation purposes. The equivalent of a moat was built around the bottom of the structure to hold back the dirt. There was going to be a grand entrance on the next level up, and the lower level was literally cut into the ground with a walkway surrounding the entire structure. This created a means for air to circulate throughout the house.

Almost all of the Natchez antebellum homes have their own folklore, and one could go on a pilgrimage tour to learn some of those stories. However, the harder stories to grasp are the stories of African Americans in Natchez during the antebellum period because those stories could not be told at the "big house."

William T. Johnson was born enslaved in 1809, but he was fortunate. His father, a slaveholder, wanted to grant him his freedom, and he was able to go before the Mississippi legislature to get approval to free young William at the age of eleven. This was during a time when more and more restrictive laws were being put in place regarding the manumission of enslaved people. It took an act of government in order for him to attain freedom. His mother and sister were also freed.

William went on to become a barber by trade and a diarist by passion, and he often played a very pivotal role in his community. He was the barber of choice for many of the "hobnobs"—the wealthy planters in the Natchez community. It just so happened that the site of the William Johnson Barbershop was on the same landmass where the Natchez Museum of African American History and Culture sits today.

William Johnson's story is outstanding because he was making a very profound statement—not unlike the statements being made by striking sanitation workers in April 1968 when Martin Luther King went to the city of Memphis. As those men picketed and protested, they carried placards that stated, "I am a man." It appeared that William Johnson went to great lengths to make that same kind of statement more than one hundred years prior.

Johnson realized that there were things that white folks could do that were not considerations for the average black man. He realized there were some who would purchase fine animals not to put to work in the fields but to race against one another. William Johnson said, "I can do that!" So he purchased horses to race as well. Johnson also realized that in order to move up in the community, one had to be a landowner. It was written that William Johnson purchased 130 acres of land for $4.12½ an acre, and then thirty days later he resold the parcel for $8.00 an acre. A black man purchasing land and selling it during these times was very unusual, but Johnson was determined to participate as much as possible in the society because he simply saw himself as a man with as much potential as any other man.

There were folks who went hunting and fishing not for sustenance but for sport. William Johnson said, "I am a man. I can do that, too!" He challenged the system repeatedly and went on to become the most affluent of the free men of color in the Natchez community in the years prior to the Civil War. He was murdered in Natchez in 1851, ten years before the outbreak of the war.

The murder was the result of a property dispute. It seemed that a gentleman on a neighboring property, hardscrabbler Baylor Winn, had been going onto Johnson's land and cutting timber that he was selling to the folks along the river. When Johnson discovered that the timber was being stolen from his land, he reported it. Ultimately, while Johnson was surveying the area one afternoon, Baylor Winn took out a shotgun and shot Johnson in the back. Baylor Winn and William Johnson were both men of mixed race. But the laws of the time stated that a person of color could not testify in any legal proceedings having to do with white folks. One of the things that Baylor Winn stressed was the fact that William Johnson had been born to a black mother and a white father. Baylor Winn argued that although he, too, was of mixed race, his lineage was a cross between white, black and Indian, and the perception was that because he was white and Indian, he was closer to being white. There were others who had been injured in the shooting, but because they were people of color, they could not testify and point the finger in court to say, "That's the man who did it!" These individuals were probably some of the slaves who were owned by Johnson. (It would have been rare for an African American to own slaves at this time.)

The trial was controversial because William Johnson was the barber who cut the hair of most of the men of substance in the community, and it was assumed that some of them would serve on the jury, but the trial itself was moved to another county. The trial went on for two years, but ultimately, since there was no one to testify that Baylor Winn did it, he got away with murder.

One of the most powerful substances ever to exist in the world, particularly in the South, is black blood. It didn't take very much of it to determine one's racial makeup. This belief became known as the Octoroon Law. A person is born with two parents, four grandparents and eight great-grandparents. The laws stated that if one of those eight great-grandparents had a drop of black blood, their offspring would be considered black, no matter how light their skin happened to be. There are stories in the Natchez community that say that although that black blood was a few generations back, and the families had at that point been named and designated as black, some of those lighter-skinned folks in later generations petitioned the court to have their racial history erased or reversed so that they could be considered white. The Barlandd family was one such family, and it was common knowledge, even to this day, that there are folks of both races who claim a link to the Barlandd name.

Because of the accomplishments that she was able to achieve, the most outstanding African American individual in Natchez was a woman of color who operated a thriving business for a period of over fifty years. Think about America, think about the Deep South, think about who ran businesses: primarily, it was white males. Females didn't run businesses. Not only was she a woman, but she was also a woman of color, so to operate a business that lasted over fifty—almost sixty—years was an outstanding achievement. She was known and respected for her philanthropic ways. If folks got themselves in a little trouble, they could go to see her, and she would pay bail to help get them out of jail. She was very giving of her resources and was a close friend and associate of many of the movers and shakers in the community.

Her name was Nellie Jackson, born in 1902. She operated a brothel that was said to remain open at least until the 1990s. She was a victim of an irate customer. She had very high standards when it came to who could come and visit her business. In 1990, she was still directing the flow of traffic in and out of the house, and when a gentleman came who had been drinking quite heavily, she turned him away. The man left but came back with some gasoline and decided he would try to burn the place down. In his drunken rage, he also managed to get a good amount of the gasoline on himself. As a result, both he and Nellie Jackson lost their lives that day. There was another brothel not far from Nellie's place, though residents have recently been trying to rehabilitate that building.

On April 23, 1940, folks had come from miles around to the Rhythm Club to hear the sounds of Walter Barnes and his swing band, the Royal Creolians. They were scheduled to play a one-night performance in the city of Natchez. For an extended period of time, Walter Barnes and his group was the house band at Al Capone's Cotton Club in Cissero, Illinois. When Capone would try to get away from the harsh winters on Lake Michigan in Chicago and head south to Florida, he would take the band along with him for his own entertainment.

Although Capone was long gone by the time of the Rhythm Club incident, the band was on its way back from a Florida tour and was making its way along the Gulf Coast. The band members had played dates in Mobile and at Mardi Gras functions in New Orleans and were making their way up to Chicago. Walter Barnes, originally from Vicksburg, Mississippi, and his band were going to stop in Natchez on a Tuesday night. After the Natchez gig, the band had plans to travel up to Vicksburg. From there, it would travel up through the Delta, on to Memphis and St. Louis and then head back to Chicago.

The Rhythm Club, a shanty-shack of a place in Natchez with tin walls and a tin roof, had an exposed-beam ceiling that had been covered with chicken wire. The gaps in between were filled with flowers and the dangling Spanish moss that hung from many of the trees in the area. Because the moss oftentimes had small bugs in it, it had been sprayed with flint, which was a petroleum-based insecticide. There has always been some controversy as to the actual cause of the fire that broke out that fateful night. Some say it was a jealous lovers' quarrel, others say it was something as common as a flick of a cigarette or a match, but the petroleum-doused moss somehow caught fire, taking the lives of 209 individuals, including Walter Barnes.

Almost every family in Natchez was affected by the tragic loss of lives from the Rhythm Club. The community lost mothers, fathers, sisters, brothers, sons, daughters, aunts, uncles, cousins, next-door neighbors, church members and co-workers. Even the white community was impacted by the loss of employees who had worked in their homes for many years.

One of the stories surrounding this tragedy involves a lady who had asked for time off because she was going to go to a big affair. Her employer told her that she was free to go, and she hung the apron on the hook by the door. She left for the party, never to return. The family, in tribute to her, kept that apron just hanging by the doorway always in her memory.

At the time of the fire's occurrence, it was the second-deadliest structural fire in the history of this nation. Today, it is listed as number seven of the top ten, and those records go back to the 1800s. We are all safer today in public places because of the sacrifices made by the 209 who perished on that evening as building and fire safety codes throughout the nation were adjusted, modified and changed. There is a museum on that site today. People will tell you that they were saved because they couldn't come up with the twenty-five cents to attend the event that night.

The Long Dream, a book by Richard Wright, was written in Paris just before he died. On the cover of the book, there is a fire scene. The story is about a place called Clintonville. This fire doesn't take place in a nightclub but in a brothel. Wright was envisioning a community where the son of an undertaker is trying to decide how to become a man. He listens to his father, and his father says, "You stand up to the white man, son." In the book, you read that he dealt quietly with the city officials. The book, of course, is fiction, but it is also folktale—this is Richard Wright's folktale about growing up in a place called Clintonville. The final escape for the young son of the undertaker is to get on a plane and fly off to Paris, just like Richard Wright did.

There are many stories about Richard Wright. He was born in a town called Roxie, just outside of Natchez. He came to Natchez on a number of occasions. There is one story that people in Natchez often retell. Wright came to Natchez in 1940 when his father, Nathan, needed some false teeth. Wright's father reportedly threw the false teeth away, and some say he threw them up in a tree because they didn't fit right. The man who now owns that property was sharecropping on it at that time. His name is Pearly Brown. It is said that Richard Wright's father's false teeth are still there on one of the trees today up on Cranfield Road in Natchez.

The details surrounding the story of the Ghost of the Kings Tavern are elusive. They say there was a woman by the name of Madeline. Tragic circumstances led to her death, and her spirit is supposedly still lurking around the structure. Any time there are sounds like the creaking of a door, it can be attributed to Madeline's presence. In the 1930s, men working on expanding the facility were ripping out a wall and found the skeletal remains of two men and a woman, along with a jeweled dagger. The woman is thought to have been Madeline, the mistress of Richard King. Richard's wife found out about the affair prior to Madeline's disappearance and ultimate death, but no one has ever been charged with the murders. The skeletal remains of the two men remain anonymous. People have walked around in the area where she is said to have frequently visited in the Kings Tavern. There has never been anything overtly creepy about the area. But the idea of feeling a cold draft of air has been attributed to Madeline. Some say that the building is merely an old structure with drafts coming through, depending on how the wind is blowing outside.

The Kings Tavern was the final stop for many pioneers traveling along the four-hundred-plus miles on the Natchez Trace. It is the oldest of the structures in the area. It was the place where people stopped to rest their weary heads, and some believe it may have once been a brothel. How old is the Kings Tavern? No one knows, but it was around during the late 1700s and is still functioning as a restaurant today.

Natchez is the last known location of the Natchez Indians. Previously, they had been at Emerald and before that at Anna Mound (named after Anna Barlow Robeson). There was a strong native presence in Natchez, followed by the French, the British and, later, the Spanish. This was before the area became a territory of the young nation. The city of Natchez has a colorful, diverse and memorable history filled with stories both old and new.

Outhouses in Rural Mississippi

It has been called a pit toilet, earth closet and honey bucket hooch, but an outhouse by any name refers to the outdoor building that houses a toilet. Talk to anyone who has ever experienced an outhouse, and they will always have a story to tell you. An outhouse in rural Mississippi was necessary when there was no water source for the toilet. Walter White said that he grew up with a one- and two-seater in his rural community before there was water, sewers and septic tanks. There would often be chance encounters with spiders and snakes. Neither creatures nor rain, snow, sleet or hail could stop one from the necessity of going to the outhouse. If the weather was really bad, one would use a slop jar in the house and dump it outside at a more convenient time. During the cold of winter, you wouldn't want to fool around. You'd go in, do what you had to do and get out.

The hole usually had a makeshift covering that served as the stool area where one would sit while taking care of business. The outhouse had a bucket of lime sitting nearby. It was used to help cover up the smell, as well as to decompose the contents left in the hole. Lots of work and time went into digging the hole and building the outhouse. Once the hole was full, a new hole would be dug, and the outhouse would be placed over that hole. Occasionally, one would have to go back and add dirt to the old hole because it would sink and settle, forming a new hole on top of the old one. Old holes would be filled up with dirt and covered with boards to keep anyone from stepping on them. The door of the outhouse had to be closed at all times, and the top had to be put down over the stool area so that cats and dogs would not fall in. Walter said that he grew up watching the advancement of his family's "throne" change for the better when they added a padded seat to the stool.

The partial moon or sun carved on an outhouse was a curious symbol that was made popular by cartoonists like Al Capp. These carved symbols on the wood frame of an outhouse are based in truth and myth. But the crescent moon symbol also filtered in the light. The moon is archetypally represented as the feminine power, the mother goddess, queen of heaven, with the sun representing the masculine force. But the outhouse theory adds a slightly different twist. It has been said that the symbols were used in communities where the people were illiterate. The sun was for boys, and the moon for girls, and there would be a separate entrance or dividing wall. The carved hole provided ventilation as well. Some outhouses had a vent pipe running from a hole up into the outhouse. It is interesting to note that the Quran refers to the femininity of shams (Arabic for "sun") and the masculinity of qamar (Arabic for "moon").

Outhouses were built close to the home, as well as in areas surrounded by trees, or on the backside of one's property. Some were found in isolated areas. There have even been a few two-story outhouses that were built near homes and could be accessed from a room on the second story. Every now and then, you could find an outhouse that had electricity, a heater or even a radio. But generally, the most modern convenience used in conjunction with an outhouse was the flashlight.

In other parts of the world where outhouses existed, the custom has been to squat over a hole in the ground. There are numerous stories of Sears & Roebuck catalogues taking up residence in outhouses and serving multiple purposes. One could read and mark the pages for future references with the possibility of placing an order later on, but the most popular use for the catalogue pages was to wipe oneself. Ser Seshs Ab Heter-Boxley of Natchez said that people were very creative in using whatever was handy to wipe oneself. People have used brown paper bags, newspaper, leaves and corncobs. Jim Walton said that he learned to read while going to the bathroom and looking through a Sears & Roebuck catalogue.

Archie Wise of Poplarville tells the story about being invited to a friend's family reunion, where all the women in attendance were pretty. They approached the outhouse talking and laughing. The outhouse was a two-seater, divided by a wall, and there was a long line of ladies waiting to get in. Archie got in the men's line, which was much shorter, when suddenly he spied the prettiest girl he had ever seen. They went in to relieve themselves at

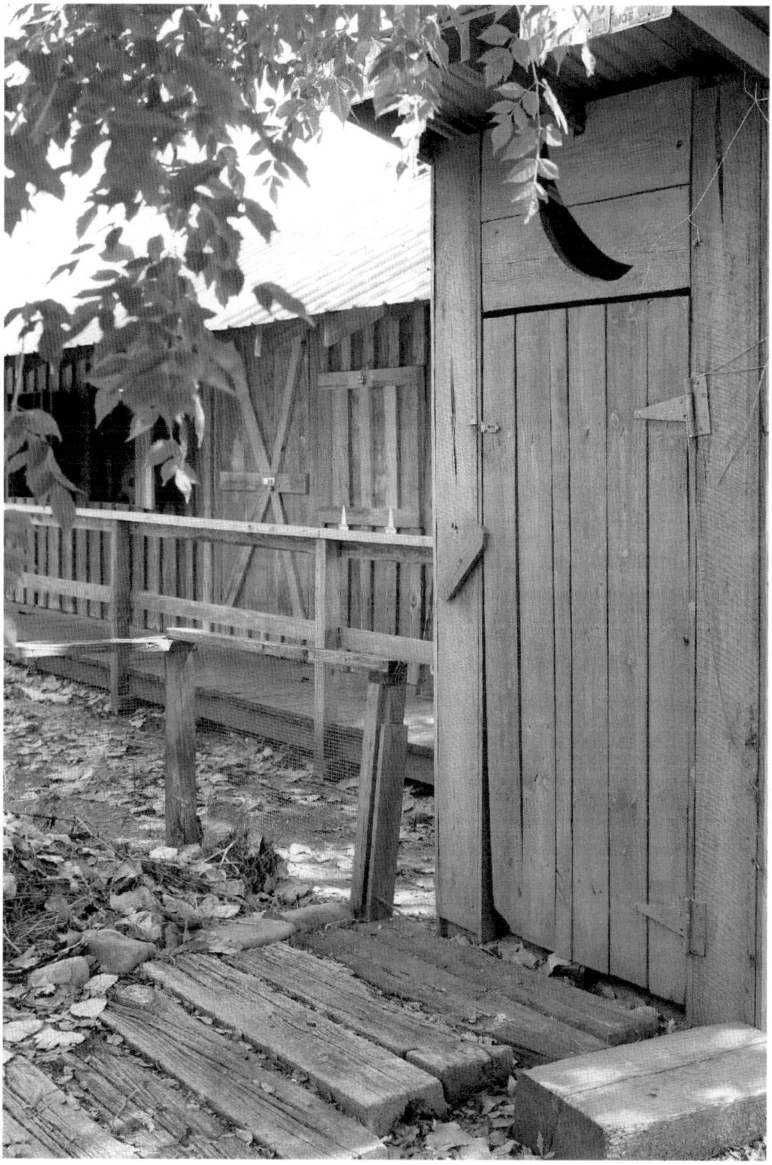

the same time, and Archie realized, as he sat there, that the girl was handing him a note under the divider that said, "You cute! We ain't kin! My name is Thelma." That's how Archie met his first wife.

Archie's grandparents had a stylish outhouse. His grandpa believed in privacy when you went to the bathroom. He had fourteen children, five nieces and nephews that he raised and two African American children who lived with him. Bathroom privacy was a gift that he gave to his family. Their outhouse had six seats, all walled in for privacy.

Hattie Gentry's daddy had a portable outhouse in Poplarville, and it had wheels. He would get the post-hole digger and dig out a hole and put the outhouse over it. When it was almost full, he would move it and plant a cabbage in its place. Hattie was asked if the family ever ate any of those cabbages. She said, "Nah, we gave them away!"

The slavery-era outhouses were situated on big plantation estates and called "privies." Antique dealers and other collectors cannot wait to get their hands on shovels when they learn of an old outhouse location from the pre–Civil War era because back then the people disposed of all kinds of things by throwing them into the outhouse. Ser Seshs Ab Heter-Boxley has dug into a few outhouse spots on the property of the Forks of the Road chattel slave market site where the Jehovah Witness Kingdom Hall now stands. He actually found some interesting items dating back to the Civil War, but who wants to prove it?

Ken Barrett's Mississippi relatives had a two-seat potty, and it was located over a creek running through the backyard, pretty close to the house, maybe seventy-five feet away from the back door. This was a strategic plan on the part of his aunt and uncle since the creek represented running water for flushing. There was one white and one red corncob impaled on a nail decorating the inside wall of the structure.

Some interesting events have taken place in and around outhouses. Occasionally, an outhouse would be turned over or set on fire by an unkind person. Kimberly Moore remembers her Uncle John and Aunt Helen's outhouse. It smelled to high heaven and always had lots of flies buzzing around. Someone told Kimberly a story about two young cousins who were playing with a friend, and they had a gun. One girl shot the young boy by accident and put him out in the outhouse pot. He wasn't discovered for a couple weeks. It was a very tragic incident.

On Halloween, pranksters would come in over the back fence at night and tip over David St. Louis's grandfather's outhouse. David's grandfather moved the building a few feet forward so that the next time the culprits attempted to push up on the building, they fell in the hole.

Irma Rockwell's grandfather loved to charm the ladies, and he loved to tell off-colored stories to his cronies. During Prohibition, he and his friends were always looking for beer. He found a source that sold it by the barrel, but he didn't know where he could store it since it was illegal and had to be hidden.

He knew of an old outhouse down by the railroad tracks about a mile out of town. It had been erected for use by the work crews that maintained the box and passenger train cars. The maintenance department had moved, and there was little use for the outhouse anymore. So Irma's grandfather and two of his friends carried the barrel of beer to the outhouse, where they placed the barrel under the hole that served as the seat. They pushed the barrel back and off to the side so it wouldn't be seen and would remain out of the waste matter as much as possible. On the backside of the outhouse, they drilled a hole for the spout of the barrel. It protruded, and the lever could be pushed to serve up a mug of golden foamy illegal beer. Neighbors were quite surprised to see men leaving the road walking through waist-high weeds every day and then holding a mug to the back of the outhouse. It was a real shock to watch as they downed the contents smacking their lips over the golden gift from the railroad outhouse. Irma said that her uncle Walter Boldt told her this story in 2007 when he celebrated his 100th birthday.

The Canton Graveyard Chase

Sandra Holmes's uncle and Mr. Kid Thompson were coming home late one night, and they decided to cross the graveyard to get home. Her uncle had on a pair of new corduroy pants. He had never paid any attention to the sound of the pants before. Just about the time the two men made it to the graveyard, Sandra's uncle heard a sound. It went, "Zip! Zip!" The two men stopped and listened and then walked faster. They stopped again, and Sandra's uncle said, "Mr. Thompson, what is that you hear?" He assured her uncle that he didn't hear anything. They kept walking, and he heard the sound again, "Zip! Zip! Zip!" The two looked at each other and picked up their pace. The sound grew faster, "Zip! Zip! Zip! Zip!" Kid Thompson said, "It's gaining on us!"

The two started walking faster; their pace was almost equivalent to a fast trot. When they made it through the graveyard and hit Robinson Road in Canton, Kid broke off and went down another road, and Sandra's uncle broke into a run toward his house. He was bailing down Robinson Road, and he assumed that whatever it was on his tail was gaining on him. He was too afraid to look back at this point.

When he got to his house, he fell in the doorway. He looked back, but he didn't see anything. He stood up, out of breath, and as he closed the door, he said to his wife, "I don't know what was chasing me and Kid, but it was going Zip! Zip! Zip! Zip!"

She said, "You got on those new corduroy pants, and the pant legs were rubbing together." He had run himself into a frenzy, and he thought that

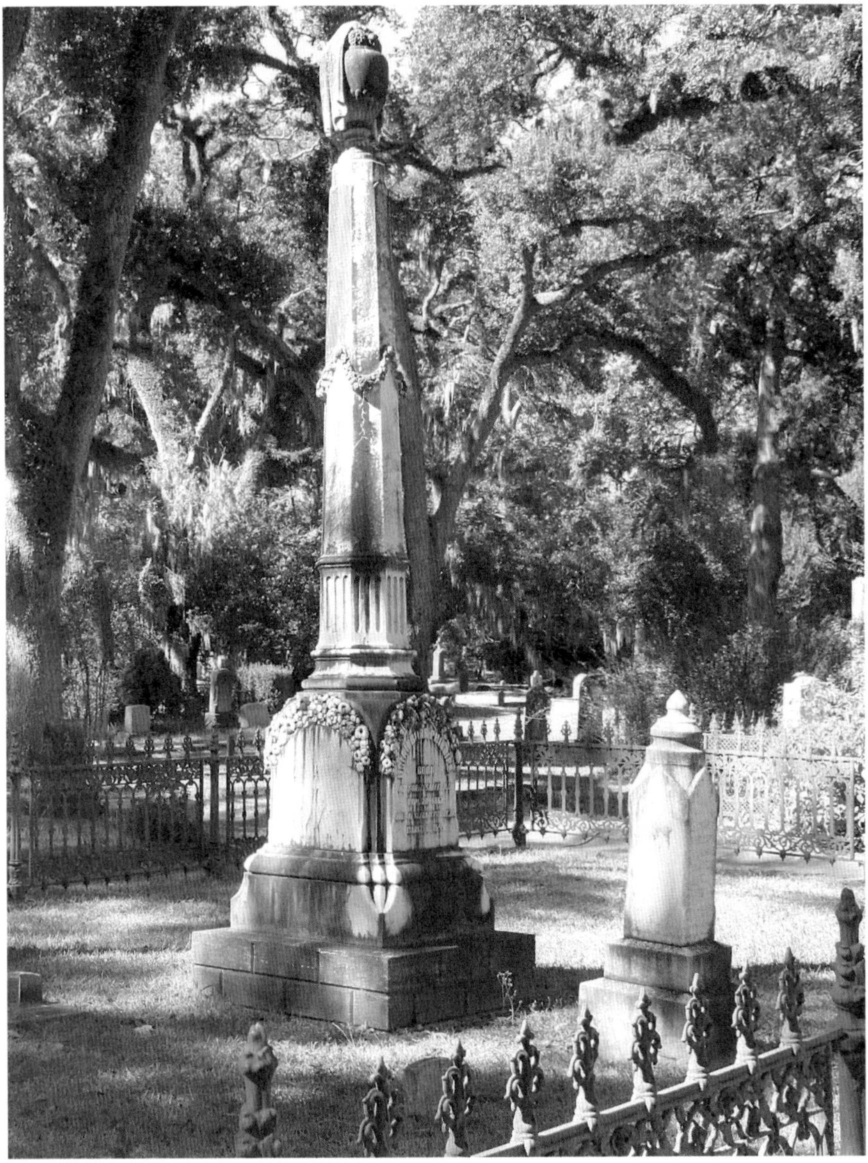

since he and Kid were making their way fast through the graveyard, there had to be something in that graveyard that was chasing them. Sandra's uncle, in retelling this story, said he almost ran himself to death.

Pretending to Be Grown in Canton

As children, Sandra Holmes and her siblings would walk to church. They had an old truck, but they lived so close to church that they walked. One evening, her auntie told the children to walk with the adults to church, but they wanted to be mature and pretend to be grown, so they walked ahead of the adults. It was windy, and there was something up ahead that looked like tissue paper in the middle of the road. The moon was shining through the trees, and they could hardly tell what they were really seeing waving about in the road. Whatever it was, it was moving up and down as if it was floating.

Trying to be brave while pretending to be grown, the children were determined to keep on walking, but when they got to the fork in the road, they became frightened. They kept seeing whatever it was ahead of them go up and come down. They didn't want to walk any farther. But Auntie said, "Now, get on up that road!"

They started easing slowly down the road. They were scared because they had heard for years that there was a ghost on that road. All the time, they had never paid any attention to what they had heard. But now, all of a sudden, all they could think about was the fact that folks had been saying there was a ghost on the road. Tissue paper, or whatever it was blowing in the wind, looked like something or somebody for sure. At that moment, the imaginations of the children had blossomed.

Sandra's auntie yelled, "You'd better get on up that road, and I'd better not catch you." Evidently, she didn't see the ghost. Sandra was frightened.

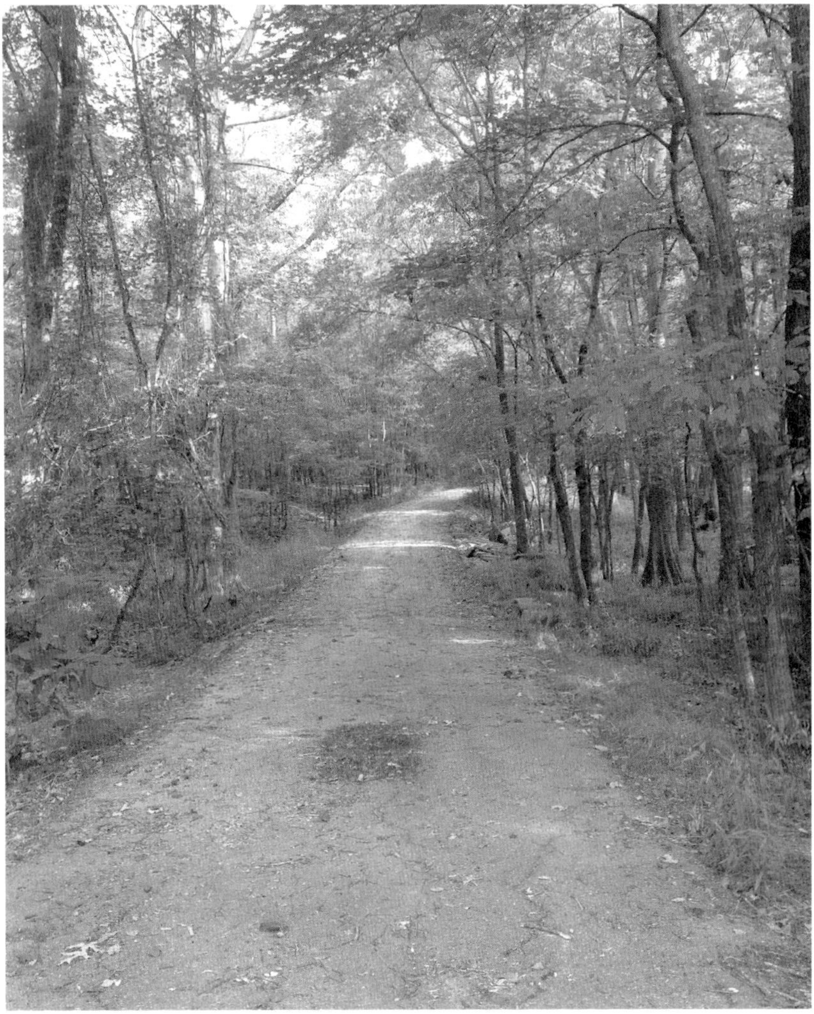

She thought to herself, "You're going to catch me tonight because I ain't going up that road."

The children saw the shadows and eased slowly toward them. Once they got up close, they ran as fast as they could past the ghost. As they ran a safe distance from it, they realized that it was just paper that strong gusts of wind kept dancing with along the path. The moon was catching it, and the shadows scared them to death. All they could glean was that it was going up and coming back down. After that frightful night, the children decided that they would happily wait to be grown.

Cooking and Eating Turtles in Rural Madison County

Start a conversation in Mississippi about eating turtles and you will soon learn that is something you probably won't want to do more than once. But at the end of the day, if you don't catch a fish, then scrape all around on the bottom of a pond, catch a big turtle with a rod and reel and then take him home for dinner. It has been said that turtle meat tastes like a cross between chicken and fish.

Generally, people who eat turtles select either the snapping or soft-shell turtles. Snapping turtles average ten to twelve inches in upper shell length and weigh between fifteen and twenty-five pounds.

Turtles are generally parboiled in their shell until the scales fall off. This makes it easier to get the meat out so that it can then be fried. The meat is parboiled first because it is said that turtles spend their lives at the bottom of ponds wallowing in rotten fish parts, decayed plant matter and all sorts of other aquatic critter poop.

When cleaning a turtle, be careful not to stab at its innards because there is a chance that you will poke into an area of the turtle that will release one of the foulest mixtures of liquid hell your senses have ever encountered.

The tabin turtle has a rounded back with polka dots on it, and it has a skirt around its tail. Some folks call this turtle "Stinkin' Jim." The tabin smells bad, and they're not good for anything—especially not for eating.

The first step in preparing to cook a turtle is the hardest because you will need to cut its head off, and this may take a little practice. One way to do that is to get the turtle to bite down on a stick and while its neck is extended

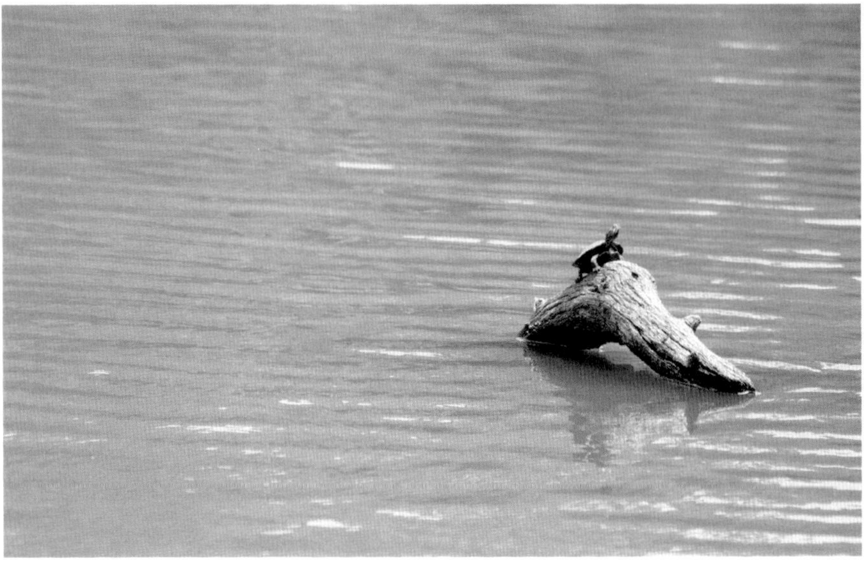

away from its body, take a hatchet or axe and cut off its head. Then you will need to hang the turtle by the tail to bleed it. There is one very important factor to keep in mind if you are going to cook a turtle: they have startling reflexes long after death.

Raleigh, Mississippi

Home of the National Tobacco Spitting Contest

Raleigh is a small town in Smith County and serves as the county seat. The name of the town is attributed to the English explorer Sir Walter Raleigh. The population in 2010 was 1,462 and was much less than that back in 1952 when the Bienville National Forest hosted its annual Forestry Field Day Festival. That's when the tobacco-spitting contest was born. It was a government-sponsored contest, and the *Smith County Reformer* wrote that it was "an opportunity to see old friends, run coonhounds, engage in a little politicking and, most of all, relish in the earthly spectacle of competitive expectoration." There was hog calling and log splitting happening at the same time on the festival grounds.

It all started when some guys cajoled one another into seeing who could spit the farthest, and a spitting contest was born. Word spread far and wide across Mississippi and then the nation, and Raleigh soon became known as the home of the National Tobacco Spitting Contest, and it held that title for many years.

There was a man by the name of Jeff Barber who will go down in infamy as the "Faucet Man." With a drizzle of tobacco juice on his jaw, when he puckered up, he was like a human faucet with masticated leaves raining out in full force. He could spit far, and he hardly ever missed. He drove up to Raleigh every year from Ocean Springs on the coast. He gained a fan base and was determined not to let them down. He once spit over thirty-three feet. The coveted prize was a gold spittoon.

Once a man from Milville, New Jersey, entered the contest and won. Folks didn't take too well to that. The year was 1976. "Yankee!" they cursed.

The preparation and qualifications for a spitting contest required that a spitting board be set up to serve as the indicator for the distance. Generally, a bronze spittoon was the target. After the aimless amber tobacco had decorated the board and the contest was over, someone took a towel and wiped down the board. It was a responsibility that few cared to take on.

The weather had to be right for a spitting contest. You didn't want too much wind blowing, and you didn't want it to rain. When the humidity was high, the spit didn't have enough velocity, and it just dropped to the ground.

There was a year when there were at least fifty folks chewing and spitting, but in time, attendance dwindled. People may have become disillusioned with the gross nature of the event, or it could have been because there was a national decline in smoking and chewing tobacco.

Festivals in Mississippi generally have names referencing fruits, vegetables and animals, such as the Potato Festival, Blueberry Festival or Great Bear Affair. Festival events in Mississippi often include a variety of diverse activities, such as pig races, monkeys riding dogs and many other surprising presentations. Musical entertainment such as bluegrass, blues, Hill Country blues and country music are main staples that keep people coming back for more year after year. Some of the most renowned performers and bands have graced festival stages, and emerging artists have learned to hold their own.

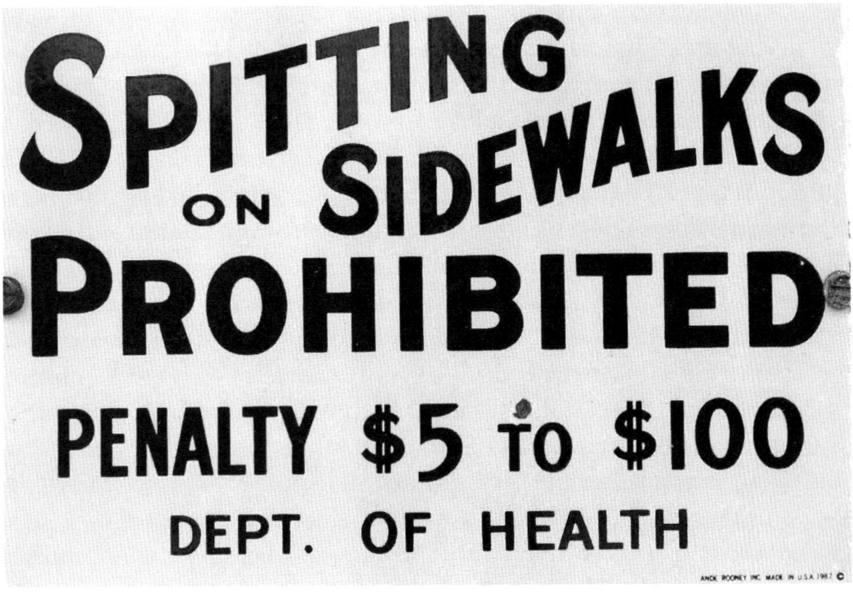

Before she became famous, country singer Faith Hill had a band, and at sixteen, she was touring community events to pay her dues. She was once booked for an appearance at the National Tobacco Spitting Contest in Raleigh, and she did indeed render a rousing performance after stepping carefully onto the stage. She feared slipping in tobacco juice residue.

Years later, she told *People* magazine, "It was so gross. They had to clean the stage off with a towel before we played."

Places Around Mississippi

What's in a Name?

Whose yo people?" and "Where you from?" are important questions to ask if you are a resident of Mississippi talking to an outsider or, as some good old country folks would say, talking to a "transplant." In the South, we have a propensity to want to connect every person to something or someone that is familiar. The smaller the community, the more inclined we are to make those connections. Without relating to something, some place or someone within a framework or reference that is common to the folk, the less apt we are to offer the hospitality that is generally extended to friends or acquaintances. With the age of computers and other forms of technology that expand our creative societies as well as our lifestyles and trends, a lot of what we have been familiar with, what has been shared and recollected from generation to generation, has become invisible artifacts. In Mississippi, when someone asks where you or your ancestors are from, we think of towns and cities both large and small, but often the names of those places have changed, and we have forgotten or family members simply don't know the stories of the places that their relatives called home.

Mississippi ranks high on the list of towns with odd names. Some of those names have changed over time, but they should never be forgotten. Some are funny enough to make you scratch your head and ask, "What were the people thinking when they named this place?"

If you want to dilute the mystery in the name, you can also look at some of the situations that marked the town. It, Mississippi, is now known as Martinsville, and you can access the town from Exit 56 on I-55. It is near

Highway 51 and the city of Wesson in Copiah County. Word has it that in the early 1800s, a man came to the area and decided that it would be a good place to settle down. He determined a certain spot along the trail would be as good a place as any to open a general store, and he went about constructing a wood-framed building with a tin roof. The work was grueling because he did it in the middle of the summer. As he hammered the last nail onto the metal roof and wiped the sweat from his brow, he said aloud, "This is it!" Ironically, "This Is It" became the name of the town. The phrase was later shortened to "It," and it remained that way until people got tired of "It" and gave "It" a more formal reference by renaming the town Martinsville. Today, there is not much more in Martinsville than there was when the town was first settled.

If you are born and raised in Mississippi in one of the rural communities, there in a sense of belonging, a relevance to staying put and a deep sensitivity to coming back if you are one of the fortunate ones to leave and come back.

The early settlers had a lot on their minds when they named some of the towns in Mississippi. Town names have created a larger-than-life interest in the folk who come from such places. Names like Africa, Alligator, Altitude, Arm, Bacon, Bullrun, Buttahatchie, Cash, Christmas, Chunky, Cold Water, Complete, Compromise, Coon Tail, Cowpen, Cyclone, Darling, Dick, D'Lo, Doglap, Eulogy, Gift, Gin, Grin, Guntown, Hardscrabble, Heartease, Hell's Creek Bottom, Hobo Station, Hooker, Hot Coffee, Hurricane, Hushpuckena, Jug Fork, Kracker Station, Longshot, Merry Hell, Midnight, Money, Moon, Needmore, Onward, Openface, Panther Burn, Possom Trot, Potlockney, Promised Land, Red Lick, Rough Edge, Sanatorium, Screwdriver, Shake Rag, Soso, Speedtown, Story, Tie Plant and Walls make us smile, laugh and even furrow our brows in suspicion as we try to figure out what people in these places were thinking.

The only time the town Nigger Ridge is mentioned today may be at someone's funeral in reference to their having been born in that town. No one calls it by that name today. But when the town was established in 1870 as the "Negro Community," the citizens were determined to have pride in their lives and their work and thereby adopted the words of Booker T. Washington as their motto: "We shall prosper in proportion as we learn to glorify and dignify labor, and put brains and skill into the common occupations of life." The town was located ten miles east of Collins, and it is the highest point in the county. Like many towns in Mississippi (Vicksburg, Ridgeland and Madison, to name a few), it was surrounded by ridges. Nigger Ridge had a unique characteristic unlike the others, however: it was shaped by a ridge that made an almost-complete circle.

Panther Burn got its name around or just prior to the 1880s. It was called Panther Burn for obvious reasons. It wasn't until the brake was being burned off that many panthers were discovered.

The town of Lux, now known as Bryant, was settled in 1867, when Joseph Bryant built a store in the southeast corner of the county. In 1900, when the Gulf and Ship Island (G&SI) Railroad came through, the citizens wanted a new name for the town and post office that reflected on its pristine cleanliness, so they settled on the Greek word Lux, meaning "light." Lux was once known for its sawmill and gin, which were built there in 1917. When the timber had been cut and the mills moved away, the town went into decline.

The origins of some of the town names often will give us a clue about the people who lived in the community. D'Lo has been given more than one explanation for its name, but it is often referenced by the fact that it is located near the Strong River, which commonly flooded, and therefore folks said that it was "too damn low." D'Lo is situated two miles northwest of Mendenhall and was founded in 1874 by W.R. May. The name "Too Damn Low" did not stick because the postal authorities would not approve the reference due to it being considered a form of profanity. Therefore, the name of the town was shortened to D'Lo. There were also a few wives' tales in reference to how the town got its name.

During the Civil War, two deserters were hanged by Confederate soldiers, and their bodies were thrown in the Strong River. Later, word spread and people started saying that the ghosts of the victims were seen along the banks of the river, so people were afraid to cross it at night.

Rocky Springs

A Place Called Home

The community of Rocky Springs was once a thriving town surrounded by a trail that led to a watering hole along the town's twenty-five-mile perimeter on the Natchez Trace. Pioneers would pass through on their way to somewhere else, and people first settled in the community of Rocky Springs in the 1790s. Around 1860, the town really took off when a station was established as a stopping place for pioneers and merchants.

Back in the early days, the only way you could find your way back through the woods to the town and out again was to mark a trail. Everyone had their way of remembering and marking the trails. Daniel Boone was known to have left his raccoon hats on trees to mark the Natchez Trace trail for others. Folks like Andrew Jackson passed by the town's watering hole during many of his trips from Nashville to Natchez with his raven-haired wife, Rachel.

Rocky Springs was a beautiful place, a world unto itself. It was a quiet kingdom where birds, insects and animals lived and played. The landscape was filled with slopes and small rolling hills, colored with shades of green, brown, orange, yellows and black. On a sunny day, the colors were vibrant and pure. The trees were lush with hanging Spanish moss and vegetation. Not only was the landscape incredible, but you could hear the water flowing from the clear spring. A walk through the woods yielded an incredible view: rocks, stones, feathers, pine straw, leaves, flowers, worms and all kinds of things blown there by the wind.

There were 2,600 people living there during the town's heyday, but there were also over 2,000 slaves who nurtured the cotton crops that made the town possible. The slaves worked nearby in the surrounding farming communities, where 54 planters and 28 overseers resided with their families.

During the early days, only a few people stopped and stayed, but nevertheless, the town grew. It had four doctors—more than most towns had around those parts—as well as four teachers and three preachers. There were thirteen artisans in Rocky Springs, and they were treated as special. Weavers spun cotton from the nearby farms. There were seamstresses who made cloth for clothing and quilts, and they even sewed the burlap bags used for carrying huge amounts of dry goods. Blacksmiths helped by making tools, horseshoes and metals that held together wagons, doors, cisterns, safes and barns.

There was even a painter who made portraits. He didn't paint houses, as color was not used on houses in Rocky Springs. The color of wood was fine enough for townspeople. But the portrait artist was special. He could capture an image much like a photographer today. People back then lived and died so young, and those portraits cemented the memories that bonded families and the community together. The portrait artist also captured the landscape on paper and canvas.

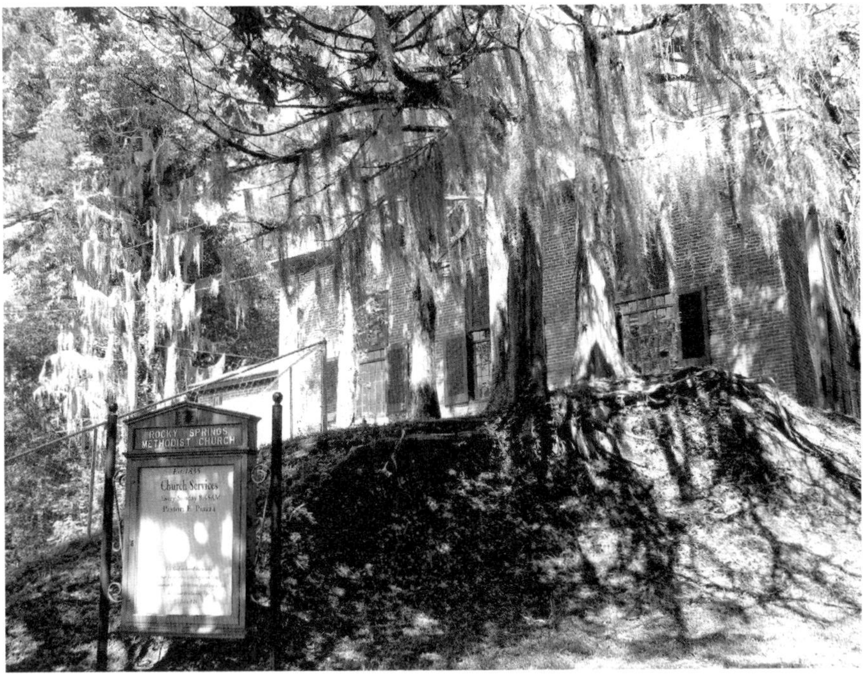

The town of Rocky Springs was once a vibrant place where people were proud to live, but the Civil War and an outbreak of yellow fever brought the town to its knees. Combined with destructive crop insects (boll weevils), poor land management and soil erosion, many died. Few lived long enough to even move away. The last store closed in 1930, and Rocky Springs became a ghost town. The population today remains at zero. All that one can find in Rocky Springs now are remnants: a few artifacts, a cemetery where the sound of buzzing bees in a hive haunt the graveyard and a Methodist church that is open to the public. Some folks still go there to pray for the mothers, fathers and babies who lost their lives to the yellow fever outbreak and for the spirit of those who struggled to maintain a sense of hope.

Windsor Ruins of Claiborne County

If you travel around Mississippi, you just might find the remnants of invisible artifacts from a time gone by. The most recognized remnants are the façades on storefronts whose worn paint gives you a long-gone glimpse of the Jewish merchant or Lebanese restaurateur's name that was either placed above the door or on the front of the top floor of a brick building that stands in a decaying town square today.

But if you veer off the beaten path, you might discover the ruins of Windsor. Ghostly and stark against a blue or gray sky, the ruins stand majestically proclaiming their long-gone youth and time-worn age, while lamenting the fiery destruction that took place before building was thirty years old.

Anyone who has ever visited or seen a picture of the huge columns that represent the ruins will soon realize the fortitude and strength of the structure whose very spirit remains on the grounds surrounding it. Windsor Ruins is located approximately five miles from Alcorn State University on a lone-bone road. As you drive down the road and come closer to the secluded wooded area surrounding the ruins, you will begin to second-guess yourself and may even consider turning around. If you are brave enough to stay the course, you will come to a rudimentary gated area. There is no security, no guard booth, no welcoming committee and no restroom. The ruins are not for the faint of heart. As long as you visit the site before dusk, the gate will be open and you can enter, though some would go as far as to say that you enter at your own risk. The wooded area is filled with trees and limbs that appear to be as old as the remaining Windsor Ruin columns.

Once you arrive at the site, there is no question that seeing the columns is well worth the trip. They stand tall against the sky. If you watch and listen, they just might tell you their story. Read the marker that is positioned on the right perimeter of the columns, and the story of the mansion becomes clear. The structure, during its lifetime, was a dwelling place for a family and included the most modern amenities for the era (late 1800s). It was built with slave labor and served as an outpost and hospital for soldiers during the Civil War.

Samuel Langhorne Clemens (Mark Twain) experienced the hospitality extended by residents of Windsor. As a houseguest, his visits were both meditative and reflective. He could often be found standing in the cupola, which was located on the center of the rooftop, and he would look out on the Mississippi River, possibly thinking of stories to write.

It has been said that a guest was on the balcony smoking and, possibly due to carelessness, may have started the fire that destroyed the mansion. The family was not at home when the fire occurred, but they returned to witness the smoldering remains of their estate.

Needless to say, gossip surrounding what caused the demise of Windsor spread like wildfire throughout the community.

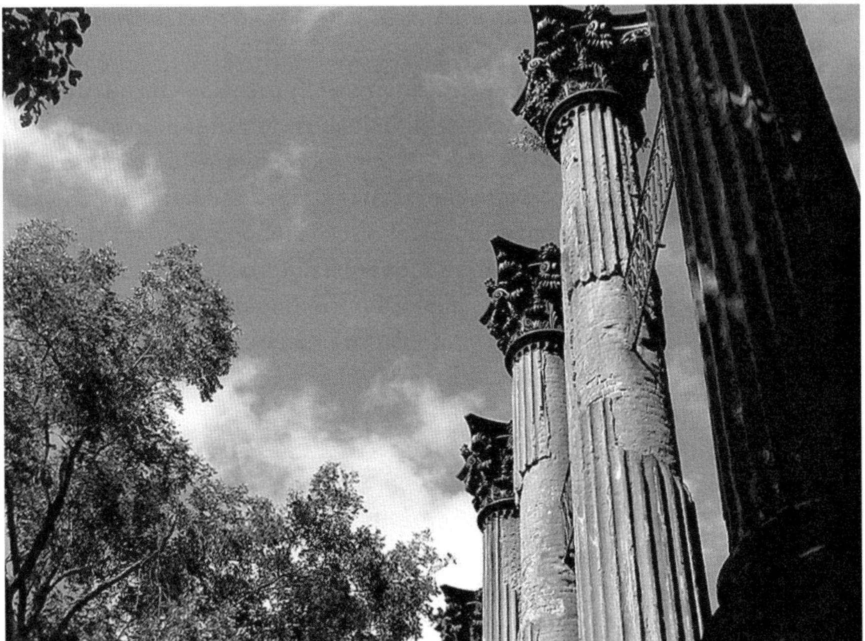

Untainted by the elements of nature and the weather, the Windsor Ruins marker reads:

> *Smith Coffee Daniell II, a successful cotton planter, completed construction of Windsor in 1861. Daniell owned 21,000 acres of plantation land in Louisiana and Mississippi. Ironically, he died in April 1861, only weeks after completing his mansion. His wife and children continued to live at Windsor but were left to suffer the loss of much of the family's holdings during the Civil War.*
>
> *Windsor's basic style was Greek Revival but with added details borrowed from Italianate and Gothic architecture. The house contained 23 rooms, with an above-ground basement, two residential floors, and an attic. The ell-shaped extension on the east side, attached to a single row of columns extending from the main square, contained the kitchen, pantry, and dining room. Rainwater stored in large tanks in the attic supplied two bathrooms. A cupola, from which the Mississippi River could be viewed, was centered on top of the roof.*
>
> *The mansion survived the Civil War only to be destroyed by accidental fire on February 17, 1890. All was lost except for the columns and the ironwork. One flight of metal stairs from Windsor is now installed at Oakland Chapel on the campus of nearby Alcorn State University. All of the Daniell family's photographs and drawings of the mansion were lost in the fire. In 1991, historians discovered a drawing of Windsor sketched in 1863 by a Union soldier in Major General Ulysses S. Grant's army. The soldier's drawing is similar to the illustration reproduced here.*
>
> *Descendents of the Daniell family donated Windsor Ruins to the State of Mississippi in 1974. Today the site is administered by the Mississippi Department of Archives and History.*

Mississippi Hoodoo

By Phoenix Savage

The following is excerpted from a longer work based on the anthropological field research conducted in Mississippi in 1996–2001 by Phoenix Savage.

Hoodoo is that odd-sounding word that could easily imply childish folly. However, hoodoo is a centuries-old tradition of magic and medical practices that were employed by enslaved Africans in North America. Long maligned for its association with causing illness and being one of many amalgamated traits of "savage heathenism" operating among rural blacks in the South, hoodoo has been denied its place within the development of African American identity and agency.

For all that hoodoo has been said to be, there are few definitive answers to the question: "What is hoodoo?" Hoodoo is often thought to be synonymous with voodoo. While not completely separate from each other, hoodoo and voodoo are not the same. Hoodoo is represented in literature dating as far back as the 1800s as a set of superstitions generally associated with marginalized rural black southerners. It has early roots in the Mississippi Delta region. The *Journal of American Folklore* (*JAF*), beyond any other publication, can be credited for the prevailing ambiguous understanding that Americans hold regarding hoodoo. This publication, while it held a mandate to publish African American folklore, did so with varying degrees of understanding and prejudice. These articles aided in the overall notion that hoodoo and other forms of what were classified as "Negro folklore" were malignant and irrational acts of African superstition. Early accounts of folklore found in the *JAF* dealing with the African diaspora illustrate this point. One of the first articles to be published in the *Journal of American Folklore* was entitled "Myths of Voodoo Worship and Child Sacrifice in Hayti." Later, in Volume 3 of the *JAF*, there appears an article entitled "Concerning Negro Sorcery in the United States." A review of the *Journal*'s index points the reader toward article titles that reflect the position of the *JAF*, namely that Negro folklore is a collection of tales commonly classified under the heading "Negro superstitions." These articles largely took the form of narratives or diffusion analysis concerned with the origin of such tales. In most cases, *JAF* folklorists believed that Negro superstitions were castoffs from European culture, which the Negros had adopted and foolishly believed in long past their European usefulness. In other cases, such tales were simply narrated with little interpretation applied, leaving the unsuspecting reader to perhaps conclude that the Negro was indeed childlike for maintaining such beliefs.

The general understanding of hoodoo is based on it being a collection of folkloric superstitions. Folklorists and other scholars who have studied hoodoo and who have, in great part, concluded that hoodoo is simply a matter of beliefs in signs or superstitions have failed to consider the role of signs within their given cultural context, as well as the particular culture's location within a society. In the case of African Americans, and in particular enslaved Africans in North America, signs were a means of communication with the supernatural world. This spiritual communication that was afforded via these signs has yet to be fully explored by scholars and has been lost within the simplistic description of "Negro superstitions."

Hoodoo concerns itself with magic and medical acts, which can be both healing and malevolent. Voodoo, on the other hand, involves rites of ritual, acts of possession, active relationships with African deities, acts of sacrifice and methods of divination, in addition to those acts associated with hoodoo: magic and healing. This is difficult for many to understand because seldom is it ever explained that those practices that make up the full body of hoodoo are also practices that are found in all the other African-based beliefs, such as voodoo, Candomble, Santeria, Obeah and Shango Baptist. In addition, the two terms are similar in sound, and since most of our data comes from locations such as New Orleans, Haiti and the Caribbean where hoodoo is lodged in these forms of African traditions as well, it often confuses the reader. The use of the word hoodoo is mainly associated with the magical/medical realm of the components that are found in the whole of all other African-derived cosmologies.

The Belzoni Lady Who Kept the Hog Hooves

There was an old plantation outside Belzoni, and the farmer who owned it had a lot of older slave women who were no longer able to farm. Many of the old women wanted to say that they were too old and weren't able to do anything. But they had the wisdom of years, and they still had the smell of the spices in their nostrils from the Motherland. They had the knowledge and the wisdom that they could share with the young men and young women. This knowledge would bring them into a time and a place that would be able to carry them over the rough times.

During hog-killing time, there was always one old lady who would be there watching and waiting to gather all the hog hooves. Folks thought it was curious that she did that. They pondered why she would gather so many. They thought surely something must be wrong with her because she wore a necklace, bracelet and anklet made with hog hooves. Something had to be wrong with the old lady because she lived in a house that had a mountain-high pile of hog hooves. Sometimes, when her window was open, depending on which way the wind was blowing or what the temperature outside might be, you could smell the odor of the hog hooves coming from her house.

The old woman may not have been able to farm any longer, but she was able to cook and teach the younger women. She was good for something! The old woman boiled a tea for everything, and she visited with the people and their children on the plantation. But people wondered if she cooked and used the hog hooves in her teas, and so they talked about the old woman.

They said, "Perhaps it must be good to wear. But it doesn't look very nice!"

"But why would she wear so many, and why is that pot always boiling on her stove?" others would ask.

The young ladies whispered, "She must be a witch of sorts. She's always cooking something. What could it be?"

One of the young women said, "I went to her house one time and she had a great big old pot boiling on the stove. I don't know what she was cooking. Do you think she was cooking humans? No, it can't be so!"

"I'll tell you what we will do," someone said. "We'll gather tonight by her window to see what the woman with the hog hooves is doing with that big pot. She's always boiling, you see."

They watched her as she began to take the dipper and pour the mixture into jars of different sizes.

"Oh my! She must have boiled them until there was nothing left," one of the women said. "Oh my, and what is that on top of the water? Surely, surely, we cannot see too clearly through the window."

The women continued trying to figure out what it was that the old woman was cooking.

"It looks kind of funny from here. Looks like the hairs from the head of those she has put in the pot," they said.

"Hmmmm! Looks funny to me!"

But the old woman kept pouring the tea. Regardless of what the young woman thought and said, someone was always coming to the house of the woman with the hog hooves for a cure.

"I wouldn't go in there, and I wouldn't drink anything that she has. I believe she is boiling humans that look like you and me," the young ladies said, as their imaginations began to take flight.

But the old woman was always saying that her tea was good for what ails you. "I don't care what ails you, you see. I don't care what is wrong with you. I got some tea for you too," she said.

One of the young ladies said, "You know, I remember when my mama was sick, I think she gave her some of that tea and it wasn't long before my mama got well, but she would never say that it was the tea that cured her. So I just don't know."

"Did she know what was in the tea?"

"No one knows for sure what is in the tea of the lady who wears the hog hooves!"

The old woman spotted the young ladies spying in her window one day, and in a huff, she began to walk. They began to move back because they imagined that she had been boiling human bones.

The woman whose mother had been cured by the old woman began to laugh and laugh and laugh, because she now realized that the old woman had helped her mother and she said, "That wasn't a human that she was boiling. That was an old hambone."

"An old hambone?"

"Yes, and that wasn't hair from anyone's head that you see."

"That wasn't the hair from anyone's head that we saw?"

"Did you see the hog hooves in the tea?"

"The hog hooves in the tea? No, but we saw what looked like hair floating on the top of the boiling pot."

"No, silly girls. I think that tea is made for whatever ails you and me. She learned the secret of putting the herbs in the hog hooves tea. I believe it is a healing medicine," the woman laughed again.

"Oh, my! I thought that she was a witch boiling human beings. Now we know. She is a medicine woman, and she makes hog hooves tea. And it helps to heal whatever ails you…whatever ails me, you see."

The woman who first realized the truth said, "Just go on down to the old woman's house. She has a great big pile of hog hooves to make more hog hooves tea."

Someone said, "I would never drink that mess, not me!"

"Well, you haven't yet got sick, sick as you can be, but she be a doctor… she be a doctor, you see. The woman that wears the hog hooves makes the hog hooves tea."

Helen Sims is a professional storyteller who remembers the stories her father told her in Belzoni. This story used to scare Helen Sims when she heard her family tell it. After her father told the story the first few times, the mystery was no longer there. It really is a story about what folks used to do with hog hooves, but the way her father told the story was to dramatize the old woman as being a strange woman using something that most people didn't know anything about: hoodoo. The older women on slave plantations were the medicine women, and when they got too old to work in the field, they did all the cooking and told the young women things to prepare them to one day know how to prepare the teas as home remedies.

The Power of the Conjurer in Belzoni

Helen Sims of Belzoni remembers so many stories that her father and grandfather used to tell. She recalls a story about the anointed women. Though a fictional story, it has some truth. It was designed to tell us a little bit about the African American culture and community on the plantation during the 1800s.

This is a plantation folktale about the spiritual women of the plantation. Every plantation had at least one. Some of them were called seers, while others were called wise old women. Many of these women were called by the name of "Aunt" or "An'tee." A lot of them were simply called old conjurers or spiritual women. But regardless of the name, they were seers who were able to discern and see things. Every time trouble was afoot, the old seer felt a sense of warning in the air.

This particular seer was the daughter of a conjurer, but she had no desire for the gift. She did not practice hoodoo—the spiritual rituals of the conjurers—but she was anointed with the gift nonetheless and was able to sense and see things before they happened. Her name was Old Lula.

To Old Lula, the gift was a curse. On this particular plantation where Lula resided, there were many things going on, and she felt the presence of many spirits. Old Lula possessed the spirit of the Motherland; she possessed a power that she herself could not shake.

When the old owl began to cry, Old Lula knew something was wrong. When the fishes in the pond began to die, Old Lula knew that something was going on. When things went wrong, many on the plantation were afraid of women like Old Lula because she was the only one who understood that the fish and owl were giving her signs that something was about to happen. No one could see what Old Lula was able to see, but when somebody on the plantation got sick, he or she would go to Old Lula, and she would mix up some herbs and make tea.

One day, a young woman named Mary came to Old Lula and said, "There is something wrong with me. I don't understand what's going on."

Old Lula looked at the young woman and said, "Daughter, you've been touched. You need some help. You don't believe in the spirit, and unless you believe in the spirit, I won't be able to help you, daughter."

Mary said, "What spirit do that be, old woman?"

Old Lula said, "Daughter, you don't believe in nothing. In order for me to help you, you're going to have to have faith that what Old Lula is about to do is going to help you."

Mary said, "I don't believe in none of that old mess. That's old stuff you talking."

Old Lula said again, "Daughter, you came to me, and you be needing my help. Now they done fed you something, and what you got in your body is poisoning your system."

Mockingly, Mary spouted, "You talk like a fool, Old Lula. I came to you for you to help me, and you telling me that somebody been poisoning me.

Old Lula looked at her and said, "The old owl be a-crying, my daughter. You are a beautiful young lady, but you've got a spirit on you. Look in the mirror, daughter. You look on yourself too good, you see."

"What you mean by that, old woman?"

Old Lula responded, "Some people stuck on themselves, and daughter, you've got to move away from the mirror. Every woman on this here plantation see what you be seeing, and daughter, you are kind of loose. You're one of them ladies who is threatening the rest of the women, and there are some women here who have another kind of spirit, and they've been putting something in your food. If you drink this tea, it will clean you out. You need to stop eating from them folks' tables because they ain't none of your friends."

The young lady told Old Lula that she was a fool and that she did not see what Old Lula saw. The next day, while folks were working in the cotton field, they could hear that old owl crying. Old Lula heard the old owl, and she came to the door. She pulled her pockets inside out on both sides of her dress and said, "Old Spirit, I'm trying to save this gal, and she don't believe in nothing. Old Spirit, help this child."

The next night, the old owl cried again. The next day, the gal went back to the cotton field to work.

Old Lula said to herself, "Something be wrong here. I'm going to try once again to talk to that gal."

She said to the young woman, "Daughter, if you drink this tea I made for you and believe that it will help you, I will be able to save you, but if you don't, there ain't nothing that I can do."

Then Old Lula went to the doorstep, and she took her shoes off and laid them upside down. She kept on calling on the Old Spirit, and she said, "Now Spirit, save this girl."

The next night, the owl was hollering and crying out again, and Old Lula said, "I ain't able to save her! There ain't nothing I can do!"

The next day, a little before noon while the folks were working out in the cotton field, they heard somebody hollering, "Help! Help! Come see about Mary here. Mary done fell out in the cotton field!"

Old Lula felt it in the wind. She began to feel a chill in the heat of the day. She said, "Y'all don't have to worry about that child cause she ain't with us no more. She gone on to the other side."

Mary didn't have faith, and she wouldn't believe in the power of the old conjurer. She didn't understand that the conjurer had a tea that was going to clean her system out.

On that plantation, Old Lula was the doctor for the folks who were sick, who believed in the ways of the old African from the Motherland. Old Lula was able to see and hear things. She was able to turn death away by putting shoes on the doorstep upside down and by pulling her pockets inside out. Every time Old Lula walked past one of them gals who had been running around wild and loose, she looked at them and said, "You got a spirit of wildness on ya. You'd better come in, gal, before it's too late." But they never listened to the spirit of the conjurer that Old Lula possessed.

When the young gals on the plantation became "knocked up," Old Lula looked at them and testified that they were pregnant before they even knew that they were. She would say, "Yeah! You be in family way, gal. You gonna have a young'un."

She once told that to a young woman who had been trying to have children with her husband for a long time. The old conjurer said, "I know that you have been trying for a long time. Bad things happened to you when you were a young gal. I am going to give you this here fish, and I done turned him belly up, and gal, you gonna be having a baby."

The man and woman laughed at Old Lula, but one thing about this young lady was different. Unlike Mary, she had faith in what Old Lula had to tell her. She said, "You know what? I believe you, old lady. I'm going to take this fish, and I'm going to do with him whatever you tell me to do because I believe you. You got the power, old lady, and I believe whatever you say will happen is going to happen."

Old Lula said, "Don't believe in me so much, gal. Believe in the great spirit that guides me. Now, you take this fish, belly up, in hand, and you do just what I tell you, gal, and you gonna be bringing a child in this here world."

Old Lula did not like the spirit that some conjurers possessed, but she was one who walked in the light, and her heart was pure. She never practiced evil rituals and spells against anyone. She only practiced the things that would warn and help people because she had the gift of discernment, and she knew the cures and remedies. She was anointed by the spirit.

There are those who have been called to help people like you and me. Old Lula believed in something beyond what you can see. She was the spirit woman, the anointed woman, the discerning woman, the witch doctor who possessed the power of the seer. Today, we have wise people, people who have the power of discernment, people who are able to tell you things, people who can see things. It is a curse for some and a gift for others. It comes from the traditions and practices of Motherland Africa.

Heed the warning! If you don't believe in nothing, and you don't have faith in nothing and nobody, then you are not able to be saved, not even by the power of the spirit of the conjurer.

The Tale of the Talking Frog and the Little Slave Boy Who Sat by the Pond

There was once a little boy who lived on a plantation, and his mama always warned him about telling other folks what the old slaves talked about. "Don't tell Massa. Don't repeat anything that you hear the old folks say because if you do, the old folks will get into trouble," she would say. Not only that, but if he told, his mama would have to leave the children, so it was important a child did not tell the things he or she heard the old folks saying.

In order for the old folks to talk about the things they didn't want Massa to know, they would steal away in the woods on the Saturday evenings when they weren't working. They would gather sticks and the pickets to make the fires on cold nights. This was an opportunity for them to talk about the things that Massa wasn't supposed to know, to sing a song that Massa wasn't supposed to hear or to share the plans they had schemed up to get over on Massa. To keep the children from revealing these secrets, they would warn the young children about a mystical talking frog with magical powers and the little slave boy who sat by the pond.

The little boy would go down to the pond every day to sit and look out upon the water. He happened to spot a frog one day. As he sat there, he began to hear a voice. When he realized that the frog was speaking to him, he became frightened. The frog said to the little boy, "You know, you come here every day. I've been watching you from afar. But if you would keep my secret, I'll give you three wishes. But you can't tell anybody that I'm a talking frog."

So every day, the little boy went down to the pond to keep the frog company by talking to him. One day, Massa's daughter spotted the boy. He appeared to be talking to himself. She asked him, "What are you doing? Who are you talking to?"

He said, "I can't tell you that, you see. It's a secret, and it is kept by me."

She said, "Aw! You're just a crazy little boy."

He said, "No, I'm not."

She retorted, "You're talking to yourself."

"No!" he said. "But it is a secret, you see."

Every day, the boy continued to meet and talk with the frog. Then one day, the little boy said to the frog, "You said that if I would keep your secret that you would give me three wishes."

The frog said, "Yes, I did. What would you have me to do? But before you make up your mind to tell me of your three wishes, think very carefully what they would be."

The little boy thought about it overnight, and he thought about it the next day, and he returned to the pond to remind the frog that he had three wishes.

The frog told him, "Remember, never speak of these things, and never tell anyone that I am a talking frog. This is a secret between you and me, and no one must ever know because if you tell the secret then you will be harmed. It is very important that you do not tell anyone."

The little boy said, "I won't tell anyone. I won't tell!"

The frog said, "In seven days, I will give you one wish, but you must not tell anyone that I'm the one who made it come true, and in seven more days, I'll give you another wish. And remember that if you do not keep the secret, great harm will come to you."

"Oh, I can keep a secret, no problem!" the boy said.

After seven days had passed, the boy wished for tea cakes baked especially for him. Sure enough, his mother said, "You have been a good little boy. I'm going to bake tea cakes for a month of Sundays."

Another seven days passed, and the boy told the frog that he wanted to be able to catch fish as big as his hand for an entire week. Sure enough, the boy's fishing rod caught fish every time it was reeled into the water.

The Massa's daughter kept watching the little boy every day as he went down to the pond to sit and talk to himself. One day, before he got his third wish, the Massa's daughter said, "I've been watching you and watching you and watching you. There is something wrong with you. You've been touched in the head. I know there is something wrong with you. You told me that you were my friend. So who are you talking to?"

He said, "Oh, but I can't tell. I must keep the secret."

She kept at him and kept at him, and finally he said, "Are you sure you won't tell anyone about my secret?"

She said, "Oh, no. I'm your friend, you see, and I won't tell anyone the secret that you tell me."

He thought about it, and he thought about it, and he finally said, "Well, I don't think I can tell you, you see. If I tell anyone, it will bring great harm to me."

"Oh, I'm not going to tell anyone," she said. "Just tell me, tell me. What is the secret that you have?"

He relented and said, "Every day, I come down to the pond, and one day, there was a frog there, you see. And the frog said that he had been watching me from afar, and I said, 'Oh, a talking frog and he's talking to me!' and I, too, did not believe it, you see.

"'Don't tell anyone that I'm a talking frog. You keep my secret and I'll give you three wishes,' the frog said to me."

She laughed and she laughed and she laughed, and said, "Oh, you silly boy, you. There is no such thing as a talking frog. You are touched in the mind."

But he said, "No, I am telling you the truth, but don't tell anyone that I told you."

She went straight away to tell everyone that he was touched in the head. She told them that he would go down to the pond every day and that he would talk to himself. "Surely, he's touched in the head. He's talking about a frog that can speak. There is no such thing."

Everyone laughed, and everyone made fun of him and said that he was touched in the head.

The people's laughter caused the boy to become defensive.

He said, "No! No! Follow me! Follow me! I will take you down to the pond, and you will see. There is a talking frog, and he does talk to me."

Everyone went down to the pond, and sure enough there was a frog there, but there wasn't just one. The pond was full of frogs.

The boy said, "Tell them! Tell them! Tell them our secret! Tell them that you are a talking frog! Tell them our secret!"

"Ribbit, ribbit, ribbit."

Everybody laughed.

The boy said, "No! No! No! No one believes me. They think I'm touched in the head. They think there is something wrong with me. Tell them, tell them, you see."

"Ribbit, ribbit, ribbit."

When the boy's mother heard about what had happened, she whipped him something terrible for sharing a false tale, and he finally made his way back down to the pond, crying. But this time his backside was too sore for him to sit down.

While whimpering, he heard the voice again. "My! My! My! You received a terrible whipping today, huh?"

The boy said, "I did. I told a secret and because of it I got a whipping, and now it is hard for me to sit on my tail."

The frog said, "Yes, I told you that great harm would come to you, and it did."

Then the boy realized that the frog was actually talking again, and he said, "Why? Why? Why in the world—I thought you was my friend! Why didn't you speak? I told them that you were a talking frog."

The frog responded, "Because the secret was yours and mine to keep. You were not supposed to tell anyone that I am a talking frog, you see. You betrayed me because you told on me, and because of that, everything that I have given to you will be taken away, and for seven years, nothing that will happen to you will be good. Not only that, but you will also never be able to hear until you learn to keep a secret."

At that moment, the boy became deaf, and for seven years, he had to learn the lesson of not telling secrets to anyone. The little boy grew and became a young man. He learned a tough lesson. Not everything is meant to be told. Keep the secrets! Keep the secrets, or pay the price of talking.

Helen Sims of Belzoni heard this story from her father, Gus Williams. Her grandfather, whom they called Papa, told the stories to her father, and he retold them to his children. Every time her family told stories, they were a little bit more exciting than the time before. Sometimes it was a little bit quicker, or a little bit slower, but that was just one story that her papa would tell that taught the children to listen to the elders and learn to keep secrets.

Stories like this were reflections on how the children ran their mouths and told everything. Helen's mama would say, "The collector is coming to collect the monies. Tell him that I'm not here."

When the collector finally came and knocked on the door to receive the payment, the children would tell him, "Oh, mama told us to tell you that she isn't here."

"Oh. Where is your mama?" the collector would say. The children would sing, "Oh, she's in the back room."

When the collector left, the children would get a whipping. The children had to learn that there were things that simply should not be repeated. It was this type of behavior that prompted Helen's parents to tell stories that taught lessons.

The Rabbit and the Turtle

Old Mr. Turtle, it seems, was the laughing stock of the community because he kept entering a race every year that he could not win. But Mr. Turtle would never give up. He would never quit. There was too much at stake. He felt that he did not have an option, and in his spirit, he knew that he would win one day.

His rival, old Mr. Rabbit, was very clever, you see. He was crafty and cunning, and he always made fun of Mr. Turtle.

Everyone in the forest said, "Oh, today, they are going to have the annual race. Who is entering this time? Surely not the turtle or the hare?"

"Oh yes, Mr. Turtle always enters the race. But who else is entering the race today?" they said.

"Well, this year we have a surprise. The frog is entering the race."

"No one is going to beat Mr. Rabbit," said the other forest critters.

Mr. Snail said that he would enter the race as well, but everyone knew that he didn't stand a chance against Mr. Rabbit. It was hard to understand why anyone would enter the race knowing that he could not win. The animals speculated that the turtle had entered the race more times than anyone else, and he had lost to the hare every time.

Mr. Rabbit was very sly. He would run in the race, but he would always go down by the walnut tree and take a nap. In the meantime, Mr. Turtle slowly paced himself along the route. No one knew that while the rabbit was sleeping, he had a friend. It was the wind, and every time the turtle got close to the tree, the wind would blow the leaves and that would wake the rabbit. Well, the rabbit was already faster than the turtle. He was crafty and he was cunning, and he uses even the wind as his friend, as well as that old walnut tree.

The last time he entered the race, the rabbit told the turtle, "Why don't you just give up? You can't beat me. You're not even designed, you see, to run in a race against me. Oh, just give up."

Mr. Turtle said, "I will never give up. I will always run the race, but one day, even you, Mr. Rabbit, will be beat."

"Not as long as I've got my hind legs, not as long as I've got my feet. There is no way that I'll ever be beat, and especially not by you, Mr. Turtle, you see."

The turtle just smiled, and he kept on running in each race. But this last time, there was something great at stake. There was the old alligator down by the pond, and he was causing Mr. Turtle a bit of trouble. Every time the turtles laid their eggs, the alligator would eat them up. This time, the alligator promised the turtle, "If you win this race, I'll leave turtle eggs alone, never to touch them again."

"Hmmm!" the turtle said. "There have been many eggs that have been eaten by you and yours, but I will beat the rabbit the next time." The old alligator gave the turtle his word that he would not touch the turtle eggs if the turtle could beat the rabbit.

"I give you my word, you see. If you can beat Mr. Rabbit, then I will never touch another egg again."

"Hmmm! That's fine with me," said the turtle. The turtle looked and he looked, and he said, "I have entered this race a thousand times, and each time the rabbit has beaten me, but this time, I must win. There is the future of the turtles at stake, and they all be kin to me. For their future, today I must win. There is too much at stake, you see. I must look to something that is higher than me."

The other animals laughed at the turtle, and they said, "He'll never beat the rabbit. It will never be. He was not designed to beat the rabbit, you see." And that was the same mindset that Mr. Rabbit had.

But this time the turtle went to a place in the forest and talked to a wishing well. He called out to a voice at the bottom of the wishing well, and he said, "I heard that you have the power, Old Wishing Well. What would it cost me to win the race against the rabbit?" The turtle stood there listening to hear what would come from the bottom of the wishing well.

It said, "I need two silver coins, and I'll tell you what to do."

The turtle replied, "But I don't have two silver coins to give to you. Can you tell me what to do that I might be able to believe that I can beat the old turtle?"

"The old turtle?" the voice said.

"Yes. Are you talking to me, or are you talking about me?"

The well said, "But did you hear what you said, Mr. Turtle? You said that you wanted enough faith to beat the old turtle."

"Did I say that?"

The well responded, "Yes, that's exactly what you said." The voice out of the bottom of the wishing well reminded the old turtle that he had to believe that he could beat the rabbit.

"You must believe that you can beat him. You have the power to beat the rabbit, but you have not really believed that you could."

The turtle said, "But I always enter the race. I enter it every time."

The voice in the well said, "But this time, you must believe with all of your mind, your soul and your heart."

"All of those things?" the turtle replied. The well said, "Yes, you must believe that you can beat the rabbit, and the power to do so will be there. You will defeat Mr. Rabbit. Are you doubting?" the voice from the old wishing well asked.

"Oh, no. I will believe! But what do I need?"

"Believe…believe…believe…" and the voice faded away.

The turtle said, "I believe. I believe. I believe." He entered the race, and everyone lined up waiting to see if the turtle would actually enter the race again with the rabbit, the frog and the snail. But this time there was something different. The old turtle had a glow on his face like never before.

The old alligator standing off watching said, "He can't beat the rabbit."

But the turtle had faith. He had entered the race one thousand times, but this time he would beat the rabbit. When the race started, the rabbit immediately ran ahead of the others. He arrived at the tree, lay down and went to sleep. But this time, the wind did not blow. It was still and quiet. The old turtle paced himself and forged ahead with all his might. It did not seem as though he could move as fast as he desired, but he believed. He remembered the voice from the wishing well that said, "Believe…believe… believe..." and he kept saying to himself, "I believe. I believe. I believe." The turtle moved closer to the place where the old rabbit slept. But this time the wind did not help the rabbit at all, for the wind was still and quiet. When the turtle was about to cross the finish line, the wind began to blow again.

The rabbit awoke and cried to the tree, "Why didn't you wake me? Why?"

In an effort to remove the blame from himself, the tree said, "It was because the wind did not blow. The wind did not blow my leaves, and therefore I could not awaken you."

Then the rabbit looked and saw that the turtle was about to cross the finish line. He ran with all of his might, but before the rabbit could make it to the finish line, Mr. Turtle crossed over. "Believe…believe…believe…," the voice from the wishing well said. "Don't say it, but believe it with all of your might. Believe with all of the power of your soul and your mind, your spirit. Believe." That's all the old turtle could hear.

The old alligator standing afar said, "I never thought it was possible for you to beat the rabbit in a race. It was never meant to be."

The old turtle said, "But you didn't know who was guiding me."

"Who's guiding you?"

"It was the power of belief. I believe it was the power of faith."

That day, the rabbit was beaten by the turtle because the turtle believed. This is another story that Helen Sims's father used to tell. It is a story of faith and impossibilities. The moral of the story is to never quit and never give up and believe all good things are possible.

A Feast Tonight!

There was a time when an old woman struggled to feed her family on the plantation. The master of the plantation would take one of the few remaining hogs and kill it for food, but there was very little left during the Civil War for the slaves. The Union army had come through, and there was only enough for the master and his family by now. All of the hogs had been killed, and there was not anything left that the master and his family had not taken for themselves. Any scraps that were left, they took to the creek and threw out for the buzzards to eat. However, this old woman believed beyond a shadow of doubt that she would be able to feed her children.

Her children cried out to her, "We be hungry! What are we to do?"

The old woman said, "Put the pots on, daughters, and start them to boil. We be having a feast tonight!"

"A feast tonight, Mama?" they asked.

She said, "Yes, daughters. We be having a feast tonight!"

The old woman looked up to heaven, and she cried, "I have believed in you and your power all my life. I've been told to trust you, and that I do," she said. "But we be hungry now, and my children and my grandchildren be needing something to eat. Master and the soldiers have taken all that's left, and all that they didn't want, they have thrown it into the creek. Master took that which was good, and the Union army got the rest. Now me and my children are here to fend and fare for ourselves."

Then the power of the Spirit of the Light spoke and said, "Those old buzzards are over there eating, and they be getting mighty full. You be saying that you be needing something. Go over there and get those innards from over in the creek bed. The heads, the feets, the tails, the yawls—take them and clean them for sometin' to eat."

She took the innards from the pigs, and she began to clean them. She took the hogs' heads, and she began to clean them. She used all the spices that she had and prepared to season everything that the master thought was not good and had thrown away. She took the hogs' heads and put them in a pot. She boiled them, seasoning them with all the spices that she had. She put the innards into a pot and boiled them unto themselves. She took the pigs' feet and the tails, and she boiled them unto themselves and seasoned them very well. And the rest of what was left, she put up in the smokehouse like the master did so that it would keep for another time.

While all the cooking was going on in the pots, the daughters were wondering what Mama was going to do with everything. When the innards were done, Mama fixed the tails, and she called the family to the table to eat. They were wondering what Mama was doing. They set there at the table full of wonder and waited on her to tell them what to do. She said, "Eat up, family, for we be having a feast tonight! If it be good for the old buzzards to eat, then all that God made is good for us to eat for they've been washed and they've been cleaned and they've been seasoned."

Mama was the first to eat, and everyone else followed her direction. It turned out to be the best meal that they had had in a long time. The old hog head had cooked all to pieces, and all the spices mixed up with what looked something like a jelly.

"Oh my, what this be?" Mama said. As it cooled down, she began to taste it. "Hmmm! This be good too!"

Later on, the rations began to run out for the old master, and he and his family went looking for something to eat.

He went to the old woman's shack, where she doled out some of her delicacies, and he asked, "What them things be called, maw?"

"They be called chitterlings."

"What part of the hog they be from?"

"Master, you might not want to know, because if you find out, you might not want to eat any more."

The old woman told this story for years, but she did not always remember the smells, the aroma or the taste. She merely remembered that once upon a time, she and her children were hungry, and because of faith, they were not to go hungry any longer. She realized that if the meat was good for the buzzards to eat and everything that the Great Spirit made was good, she just had to season and cook it, and she and her children could eat it.

People from all over have been eating chitterlings, hogs head cheese, pigs' feet, tails and ears. Of course, people ate these things in other communities, but this was the first time that this old woman and her community had done it. Where she was from, they usually threw that stuff away, but not this time. It became a necessity to eat it, and it gradually became recognized as a delicacy fit to be called a feast.

In Louisiana, they use all of the hog, including its hair to make brushes. They drain the blood. But there is even a ritual for using the forbidden blood of a hog. Eating pigs' tails, feet, ears, heads and innards was not practiced widely among all slaves. That may be why the old woman said, "I might better not tell you where this food came from because you might not want to eat it if you knew."

After Helen's daddy told this story to get her and her siblings to eat pork, she responded by saying, "Daddy, you can dress that one up any way you want to, but I ain't fixing to eat no chitterlings."

ACKNOWLEDGEMENTS AND NOTES

Ivory-Billed Woodpeckers in Madison County

Lyle Wynn has been a practicing blacksmith for over fifteen years. He is a third-generation blacksmith, and the art of metal is in his blood. Lyle is a member of the Craftsmen's Guild of Mississippi, and he is listed on the Mississippi Arts Commission's Artist Roster. He resides in Brandon, Mississippi.

Frog Gigging in Rolling Fork

Upon introduction, Tommy Shropshire says that his name is spelled like the Shropshire Lad, a series of sixty-three poems by the English poet Alfred Edward Housman (1859–1936). He went on to say that there is a Shropshire, England. In his best southern drawl, he added one more declaration and stated that his name is also a breed of sheep. Even though Tommy Shropshire grew up in the Mississippi Delta, he now lives in the Jackson area. He retired in 1999 after thirty years of working with Mississippi Wildlife Fisheries and Parks.

Old Jim Gordon's Gold in Willoughby and The Gunfight at Willoughby Crossing

Ralph E. Gordon is a fifth-generation Mississippian who has always had a passion for history, especially relating to his family. Since his retirement from sales in 2005, he has devoted himself to researching and writing about family and Mississippi history. He is past president and still active in the Mississippi Writers Guild. Ralph is a musician, nonfiction writer and poet. He lives in Union, Mississippi, with his wife, Pat.

The Ghost Train of Little Rock

The poem "The Ghost Train" is a legend in verse. In July 2013, Ralph E. Gordon, the author of this story and poem, had a conversation with a one-hundred-year-old gentleman who grew up in the Little Rock community. His mind and distant memory were sharper than those of many younger people. He told Ralph that in the early part of the twentieth century, the fare from Little Rock to Meridian was twenty-five cents. A nickel would get you a ride from Little Rock to Union.

Ralph E. Gordon's article about the doodlebug from Little Rock to Meridian appeared in the *Journal of Newton County Historical Society* (2013). Much of his information was gathered from older members of the community and from his grandfather Howard Kirby, who worked for the M&M and the GM&O.

How Poplarville Got Its Name

The name of the town of Poplarville is associated with the national attention on the town of Poplarville in 1959. In April of that year, Mack Charles Parker, an African American man, was accused of rape. He was abducted from the jailhouse in Poplarville by a mob and shot to death. His body was later found in the river. No one was ever prosecuted for the crime. This brought attention to the community as it marked one of the last documented lynchings in our country and helped to accelerate the American civil rights movement. We should never forget tragedies like this, but we should look deep in the hearts of our communities to find what is good, wholesome, common, traditional and worthy of celebrating. Mississippi has had to overcome a lot when it comes to its history and its stories, but it is a beautiful state with so much to offer its residents, visitors and newcomers. The people are proud and want to show it off to everyone and beg not to be judged by something that they continue to ask forgiveness for.

Poplarville Has a Haunted House

Mary Etta Moody is a professional storyteller living in Poplarville. She has an uncanny talent for remembering the most important details and descriptions of history and community, and if she says she felt the presence of a ghost, then there is no doubt. Mary Etta is originally from Bogalusa, Louisiana.

In September 2013, WJTV reported that El Chupacabra was spotted and killed in Pigtown, a community in Lena, Mississippi. It had glowing red eyes and it "ran funny like its front end was lower than its back end. The animal's nails were longer than that of a dog," according to the news report. In October 2013, WLOX in Pearl River County ran the headline "Mysterious Creature in Picayune Resembles 'El Chupacabra.'" Picayune is less than twenty miles from Poplarville. Ghost or wild dog, there is always a logical explanation for sounds that go bump in the night.

Mary Etta Moody was also instrumental in telling the stories in the following chapters: Marijuana and Moonshine, Murder Creek, Midwifery and The John Ford House. She is a member of the Poplarville Storytelling Guild.

The Big Chicken Fight in Wiggins

It has been said that okra comes from the upper countries in Africa (Ethiopia), and it is also known to have grown in some West African countries. Mississippi has okra native to its soil. It has a button on it. Some say it isn't good to eat, but it is. Okra has also been called lady's fingers.

Bill Restor is a local resident and storyteller who has a lot of stories to tell about the life and times of living in Wiggins. He is a member of the Poplarville Storytelling Guild. Bill Restor was also instrumental in telling the stories in the following chapters: How Poplarville Got Its Name; Bill Restor's Childhood Possum; Murder Creek, the County Crossroad; and The Turpentine Shack in Pearl River County.

Milking Cows in Carnes

Ernestine Thompson is a resident of Carnes, Mississippi. She tells a story from her childhood of milking cows, but most of her stories relate to her Native American ancestry.

The Wiggins Pickle Factory

Rita Restor is on the pickle factory museum committee, which is working to document this history. She is the wife of Bill Restor and resides in Wiggins.

Marijuana and Moonshine in Poplarville and The Two-Dollar Mule in Aberdeen

Douglas H. Strahan lives in the Poplarville community. He is a retired federal and customs agent and a veteran who has worked in several branches of the military. He is a member of the Poplarville Storytelling Guild.

Midwifery in Sandy Hook

During the tough times in Mississippi's history (mid- to late 1800s) and immediately after Emancipation, the African American midwives were able to make a living when others were struggling to exist. That should never be forgotten. They transcended black and whites, class and income. They nurtured babies, took care of mothers' homes and became an integral part of what sustained the family until the mother could get back on her feet. When a person lived far out in the country, it may have been too far for the family to get to the doctor in time for the delivery, but the midwife always found a way to make it to the family home. A black midwife was an asset to her community during a time when African Americans were impoverished. A midwife went beyond just delivering babies, and by the turn of the twentieth century, her role was considered honorable. This story is a recounting of Mary Etta Moody's great-great-grandmother's life.

The John Ford House of Sandy Hook

Mary Etta Moody is a direct descendant of Reverend John Ford.

Keep Okolona Hummin'

The people in Okolona have shared the song "Keep Okolona Hummin'" for many years. It is their theme song. Okolona started out as a settlement in 1845. The postmaster from a nearby development knew of the Chickasaw brave Oka-laua, and he named the town Okolona in his honor. The brave's name means "peaceful yellow or blue water." In partnership with Patsy Gregory of the Okolona Chamber of Commerce, myself and Rebecca Jernigan collected the stories along with and for the residents of the community.

Love Is Like Cornbread: A Story of Unconditional Love in Columbia

The nucleus of this story was told to me by a resident of Jackson, Mississippi. She said, "My great-grandfather lived in Columbia. He was eight feet tall. He left one day, just walked out on the family. Went off into the woods and wasn't seen again for two years. When he came back, no questions were asked. The family was just so glad to see him." I envisioned a story of unconditional love, and I was compelled to write the rest of the story as I imagined it. I told this story in South Mississippi once, and a woman in the audience frowned at me throughout the telling. Afterward I introduced myself to her, hoping to get a sense of what caused her to look so perplexed. She gladly responded that she knew a man in Columbia who stood eight feet tall, but clearly it was a different person. I laughed and said, "I wonder what kind of milk they've been drinking down there!"

The Corinth Railroad Story

On May 10, 1869, the Union and Central Pacific Railroads joined their rails at Promontory Summit, Utah Territory, connecting the rail system across America. More information can be found at: www.nps.gov.

Natchez: Back in the Day

Darryl White, executive director of the Natchez Museum of African American History and Culture, and David Dwyer, originally from Indiana and now living north of the town of Natchez, both know the stories and history of Natchez and sat down to be interviewed. Later on in the interview, we were joined by Jeremy Houston, who is a volunteer/intern at the museum and has joined the museum's research team.

The Canton Graveyard Chase and Pretending to Be Grown in Canton

Sandra Holmes is a member of Fellowship Bible Church, where she attends weekly services. She is a local latch-hook rug designer and quilter.

Mississippi Hoodoo

Phoenix Savage is a visual artist and Fulbright Fellowship recipient. She has contributed scholarly research to several encyclopedic entries, and her scholarly work is based on ethnographic research of southern black culture exploring hoodoo, civil rights, African spirituality and contemporary black health.

The Belzoni Lady Who Kept the Hog Hooves, The Power of the Conjurer in Belzoni, The Tale of the Talking Frog and the Little Slave Boy Who Sat by the Pond, The Rabbit and the Turtle and A Feast Tonight!

Helen Jean Sims is known as the "Old Storyteller." She travels the state sharing her tales and reenacting episodes from American history relating to slavery, the Civil War, sharecropping, blues and gospel music and the civil rights movement. Her stories are based on authentic facts and are rich in African and African American cultural heritage. Helen is on the Mississippi Arts Commission's Artist Roster. She is one of the few individuals in the entire state who vividly remembers the stories that her father and grandfather used to tell the children.

Additional Contributors

Ken Barrett, Lorraine Craig, David Dwyer, Hattie Gentry, Ser Seshs Ab Heter-Boxley, David St. Louis, Kimberly Moore, Irma Rockwell, Jim Walton, Darryl White, Walter White, Archie Wise and Brinda Willis.

Bibliography

Al Capone: The Music He Lived and Died By. Various artists. Master Classics Label, 2008.

Bascom, William Russell. *African Folktales in the New World*. Bloomington: Indiana University Press, 1992.

Bearss, Margie Riddle. *Sherman's Forgotten Campaign: The Meridian Expedition*. Baltimore, MD: Gateway Press, 1987.

Booth, Dottie. *Nature Calls: The History, Lore, and Charm of Outhouses*. Berkeley, CA: Ten Speed Press, 2008.

Campbell, James. *Exiled in Paris: Richard Wright, James Baldwin, Samuel Beckett, and Others on the Left Bank*. Berkeley: University of California Press, 2003.

Caron, Peter L., Jr. *Morse Code: The Essential Language*. N.p.: American Radio Relay League, 1996.

Coleman, Jerome, and Loren Coleman. *Cryptozoology A to Z: The Encyclopedia of Loch Monsters, Sasquatch, Chupacabras, and Other Authentic Mysteries of Nature*. New York: Fireside, Simon & Schuster, 1999.

Cuhaj, George S. *Confederate States Paper Money: Civil War Currency from the South*. Iowa, WI: Krause Publications, 2012.

Davis, William C. *A Way through the Wilderness: The Natchez Trace and the Civilization of the Southern Frontier*. New York: HarperCollins Publishers, 1995.

Dickerson, James L. *Faith Hill: The Long Road Back*. N.p.: Sartoris Literary Group, 2012.

Dray, Philip. *Capitol Men: The Epic Story of Reconstruction through the Lives of the First Black Congressmen*. Chicago: Houghton Mifflin Harcourt Publishing Company, 2010.

Ehrenreich, Barbara, and Deirdre English. *Witches, Midwives and Nurses: A History of Women Healers.* New York: Feminist Press, City University of New York, 2010.

Foote, Shelby. *The Civil War: A Narrative: Fredericksburg to Meridian*, Vol. 2. New York: Random House, 1963.

Foster, Buck. *Sherman's Mississippi Campaign.* Tuscaloosa: University of Alabama Press, 2006.

Fricke, Pierre. *Confederate Currency.* New York: Osprey Publishing, Limited, 2012.

Gallagher, Tim. *The Grail Bird: Hot on the Trail of the Ivory-Billed Woodpecker.* Boston/New York: Houghton Mifflin Company, 2005.

Gandy, Joan W., and Thomas H. Gandy. *Natchez: City Streets Revisited.* Mount Pleasant, SC: Arcadia Publishing, 1999.

Garbo, William. *Windsor Ruins: A Plan for Historic Site Development, Claiborne County, Mississippi.* Jackson: Mississippi Research and Development Center, 1973.

Harris, Jessica B. *High on the Hog: A Culinary Journey from Africa to America.* New York: Bloomsbury, 2011.

Housman, A.E. *A Shropshire Lad.* Mineola, NY: Dover Publications, Inc., 1991.

Hurston, Zora Neale. *Mules and Men (Appendix I: Negro Songs and Music).* New York: Harper Perennial Modern Classics, 2008.

Johnson, William, William R. Hogan, and Edwin Adams Davis. *William Johnson's Natchez: The Ante-Bellum Diary of a Free Negro.* Baton Rouge: Louisiana State University Press, *1993.*

Kreck, Dick, and David Fridtjof Halaas. *Hell on Wheels: Wicked Towns along the Union Pacific Railroad.* Golden, CO: Fulcrum Publishers, 2013.

Lamb, J. Parker. *Railroads of Meridian (Railroads Past and Present).* Bloomington: Indiana University Press, 2012.

Leckie, Shirley A., and William H. Leckie. *Unlikely Warriors: General Benjamin H. Grierson and His Family.* Norman: University of Oklahoma Press, 1998.

Lynch, John R. *The Facts about Reconstruction.* Middlesex, UK: Echo Library, 2007.

Marrin, Albert. *Old Hickory: Andrew Jackson and the American People.* New York: Dutton Children's Books, Penguin Young Readers Group, 2004.

McCall, John B. *The Doodlebugs.* Derby, KS: Santa Fe Railway Historical & Modeling Society, 2002.

McDowell, Dr. Gary D., and Ruth A. McDowell. *Mississippi Secrets: Facts, Legends, and Folklore.* N.p.: iUniverse, Inc., 2007.

Moore, Edith Wyatt. *Natchez Under-the-Hill.* Natchez, MS: Southern Historical Publications, 1958.

Morgan, Speer. *Frog Gig and Other Stories (A Breakthrough Book).* Columbia: University of Missouri Press, 2010.

Outland, Robert B., III. *Tapping the Pines: The Naval Stores Industry in the American South.* Baton Rouge: Louisiana State University Press, 2004.

Pembleton, Seliesa. *The Pileated Woodpecker.* Minneapolis, MN: Dillon Press, 1989.

Pritchard, William Thomas. *This Is Magic: Secrets of the Conjurer's Craft.* New York: Citadel Press, 1957.

Radford, Benjamin. *Tracking the Chupacabra: The Vampire Beast in Fact, Fiction, and Folklore.* Albuquerque: University of New Mexico Press, 2011.

Rowley, Hazel. *Richard Wright: The Life and Times.* Chicago: University of Chicago Press, 2008.

Rowley, Matthew. *Moonshine!: Recipes * Tall Tales * Drinking Songs * Historical Stuff * Knee-Slappers * How to Make It * How to Drink It * Pleasin' the Law * Recoverin' the Next Day.* Asheville, NC: Lark Crafts, 2007.

Shepherd, David, and William K. Plummer. *We Were There at the Driving of the Golden Spike.* Mineola, NY: Dover Publications, 2013.

Smead, Howard. *Blood Justice: The Lynching of Mack Charles Parker.* Oxford: Oxford University Press, 1988.

Stevens, Janet. *The Tortoise and the Hare: An Aesop Fable.* New York: Holiday House, 1985.

Tanner, James T. *The Ivory-Billed Woodpecker (Dover Birds).* Mineola, NY: Dover Publication, Inc., 2003.

Twain, Mark. *Life on the Mississippi.* 1876. Reprint, Simon & Brown, 2011.

Whitington, Michel. *A Ghost in My Suitcase: A Guide to Haunted Travel in America.* Dallas, TX: Atriad Press, 2005.

Websites

Boxley, Ser Seshs Ab Heter-Clifford M. "Forks of the Roads." www.forksoftheroads.net.

City of Okolona. "Carnegie Library." www.cityofokolona.com/library/index.html.

Cornell Laboratory of Ornithology. "Exploring and Conserving Nature: The Search for the Ivory-Billed Woodpecker." http://www.birds.cornell.edu/ivory.

"The Ivory-Billed Woodpecker: Is He Still Here?" www.ivorybill.org.

"King's Tavern." www.ghostinmysuitcase.com/places/kings.

"The King's Tavern." www.hauntedhouses.com/states/ms/kings_tavern.htm.

Olmstead, Alan L., and Paul W. Rhode. "Wait a Cotton Pickin' Minute!: A New View of Slave Productivity." http://www.history.upenn.edu/economichistoryforum/docs/olmstead_07.pdf.

The Rhythm Club Fire. Official website for the documentary film. http://rhythmclubfire.com.

"Walter Barnes: The Natchez Fire." www.weeniecampbell.com/yabbse/index.php?topic=8746.0.

WBEZ91.5. "The True Story of Natchez Burning." www.wbez.org/episode-segments/true-story-natchez-burning.

About the Author

Diane Williams is a program director for the Mississippi Arts Commission, a statewide arts and service organization, and she currently resides in Mississippi. She has been a professional storyteller since 1992 and serves as a board member for the National Association of Black Storytellers. She is a former board member and former board chair for the National Storytelling Network. She is author of several books and poems, and her work has appeared in numerous literary journals. Diane is also a mixed media fiber artist whose work has appeared in museums and galleries through the state of Mississippi. She jokingly describes herself as a "narratologist," stating, "It's all about the story!"